D0984311

Dancing with Minnie the Twig

www.**booksattransworld**.co.uk

DANCING WITH
MINNIE THE TWIG

Mogue Doyle

BANTAM PRESS

LONDON · NEW YORK · TORONTO · SYDNEY · AUCKLAND

FIC
D7546da

TRANSWORLD PUBLISHERS
61–63 Uxbridge Road, London W5 5SA
a division of The Random House Group Ltd

RANDOM HOUSE AUSTRALIA (PTY) LTD
20 Alfred Street, Milsons Point, Sydney,
New South Wales 2061, Australia

RANDOM HOUSE NEW ZEALAND LTD
18 Poland Road, Glenfield, Auckland 10, New Zealand

RANDOM HOUSE SOUTH AFRICA (PTY) LTD
Endulini, 5a Jubilee Road, Parktown 2193, South Africa

Published 2002 by Bantam Press
a division of Transworld Publishers

A catalogue record for this book is available from the British Library
ISBN 0593 049233

Typeset in 12/16pt Granjon by
Kestrel Data, Exeter, Devon.

Printed in Great Btitain by
Mackays of Chatham plc, Chatham, Kent

1 3 5 7 9 10 8 6 4 2

Dancing with Minnie the Twig

1

THE BELL STRIKES; THE CHURCH SHAKES.

Vibrations fill the mountain village and spread beyond: out over the hall and on across Murphy's fields. At some point along the way, the sound loses its clanging and clanking and grows easier on the ear till, farther out, it changes into a pleasing sort of chime – almost musical. It goes out over Patsy Doran's vegetable plot, down along the valley, across the river and up the other side, past Mrs Rourke's house and our place; then over to where little Mikey Doyle lives – the house in the fields. And away, till it fades in the evening air over the flat townlands, where the big farmers live and the fat hangs off the cattle in the long grass.

Mogue Doyle

When the bell strikes, few other things around here are more important: it must be obeyed. In school at twelve o'clock, right on the dot before the second gong goes off, the master and our class rise to our feet in the same big wave-burst, everything dropped . . . Clang! I am the bell. Stop what you're doing right now. I am what matters most; listen to me. Come with me from this place and float with my chimes in the air, over the valley, across the flatlands and away, along to another valley the same as this one.

But, as anyone round here will tell you, the best place to listen to the bell is up the Blackstairs mountain, and the farther up the better, where the sound closes in, not by dribs and drabs on the wind but piercingly, like a baby's yells in the middle of the night. Come Fraughan Sunday in July, six o'clock in the evening, we all straighten our backs and stand rigid till the ringing dies away. We wrap calico tablecloths, or whatever was quickest to hand at home that morning, round bundles of fraughans, bits of heather and stalks of grass, and plonk the lot into brown baskets. It's usually a race then, down the sheep paths and round the heather that scratches our bare legs, with our mad-dog shouting to pick up where the ringing left off. Fecking mountain! It would tear the legs of a young fellow without long trousers.

It's not a bad old mountain all the same. It has a great colour: deep purple, the exact same as the tart Mam makes from the fraughans I bring home – blueberry pie, she says, they call it over in America. The way the mountain range curves up and down, in big rolling sweeps, makes it easy on the eye; not like those great pointed needles you'd find in a magazine, scary-looking things. From up there, on a clear day in September, it's possible to pick out the Tower of Hook to the far south, the Wicklow Mountains to the north and, eastwards, the coast – only on a very fine day, mind. The flatlands of Carlow, good scallion-eating country, stretch away westward to the marble city of Kilkenny, where the game of hurling is only mighty.

Right under where the gap in the range is biggest and the sweep is at its lowest, my village sits on a shoulder, like a loose slate about to slide down a sloped roof and drop on someone's head. There's the hall, where the pictures are shown on Wednesday and Sunday nights. Murphy's own most of the village: the pub, the shop, three or four houses and the farm beside the church. The church, the tallest building in the place – despite competition from Murphy's hayshed nearby – sits tucked in against the butt of the hill. A path runs around its three sides, and all the graves are outside of that: a garden-ful of headstones and tombstones. Another path goes from the church door, through the graves, to the street. One long village street. Round the bend, at the far end of the street, is the school, Master Mooney's territory. And instead of headstones for a garden, it has rows of grass and dandelions shooting up through the concrete, dividing the playground into patches. I could walk that place with my eyes closed, especially those steps leading down to the backyard where the shelter is. Codd's house beside the school is at a much lower level.

When the bell rings, Murphy's dog sticks his head in the air and starts to howl. His moaning, like the mountain range, rises and falls with each clang, and ends only when the ringing ends. That fellow is as old as the hills, and nobody round here can recognize what breed he is. I can't remember a time when he wasn't mangy, or didn't have a scabby backside with his magairle puffed out. Yet his tail is always in a loop over his back. A pure beggar, he's forever outside Murphy's shop, waiting for tidbits from people, and likes to have his food handed to him, mind you: won't touch any scrap just thrown on the ground. A wooden block, one time, had to be tied from his neck; he'd taken a fit of chasing cars passing on the street. That soon changed his tune, knocking the bad habit out of him. The block was removed though, because it was dinting the doorway every time he went into the pub. When missing from outside the shop, he's usually in the pub next door: wide eyes staring up into old lads' faces, looking for porter. All the same, there's something likeable about the mangy old brute. Maybe it's because he's as much part of this place as the schoolyard, the graveyard, the mountains and . . . It's my place, and I like everything that goes to make it up. Well, almost everything.

In our village, the priest's housekeeper, old Mrs Brennan, is the bell woman. It's great watching her in action. Out she comes, always at the right minute, tearing along the pebblestone path from the priest's house to the side. Out through the gap in the high hedge and up to the church gable, at such a pace as might take her through the wall without stopping, though she always manages to pull up in the nick of time. Black dress, black stockings, black shoes and a black hat over a grey bun. Sergeant Major Mrs

Brennan unties the rope knot and starts to tug downwards, unleashing an almighty power. Her knees bend, her hump sticks out and she is off pulling like a Trojan. The clapper falls, the bell clangs again and the village shakes. One of these days, that woman will have the church gable down round her ankles. Without Mrs Brennan, time in this place would surely stand still.

This evening the bell is ringing for a funeral. Right now, that funeral – a hearse, the crowd walking and two black hackney cars behind – is no more than a couple of hundred yards from the village. Most of the people who are not walking behind the hearse have already arrived here in the street, and are waiting. Old women in black, who love occasions like this, stand outside the church door at the end of the path through the headstones. The men stand in twos and threes chatting along by the wall, on the street foot-path. I'm going to go over to one group, where there's bound to be some bit of a laugh.

Heading into the bad weather again, men, are we? says one fellow.

Surely not looking the best this evening anyway, says another.

Are you blind or what? I say to them. The sun is shining: is that not good enough? But they just ignore me. Always the same story around here: nobody wants to listen to what young lads have to say.

The rain's not too far off anyway, says Long Bob; the mountain she looks horrid near. He turns the head sideways to check the Blackstairs over his shoulder. You'd think the Blackstairs was going to move in and give him a clatter, the way he cranes his neck, looking back. Horrid near! When did Bob ever before notice anything, whether it was *horrid near* or not; except for, maybe, a basin of boiled spuds sitting before him on the table. Talk about eating! The man was born to eat; still not a pick on him to show for it. Eating, and then chasing young lads out of his yard: lads like us, who'd only ever go in there to get back their ball. Well, that's Long Bob for you.

Oh no, the bogey-man himself has just landed. Patsy Doran comes strutting like a hen – more like a fecking bantam cock – across the street on to the path, and joins the group. See how careful he was, the way he parked his nice grey Anglia. How long has he got that one for now? That fellow had a car when nobody else in the area had one. Has to be said, he thinks more of that old jalopy than he does of anything or,

for that matter, anybody else. Just look at the grey leather seats and the dash: he has them spick and span, boy. Wouldn't I love, right now, to get my hands on that steering wheel and go vroom-vrooom up and down the street. Hey lads, would yous like a spin in my new car? Sorry, I've changed my mind; I don't give lifts to mangy old fellows who refuse to listen when I've something to say. Then I'd drive like hell through the next county; with nobody for company but Murphy's scabby-arsed dog, sitting up in the front seat, checking every village we'd pass through for church bells to give out to. Off we'd roar as far as Kilkenny to watch a mighty game of hurling; then drive through those marble streets, and we'd not come home till the small hours, headlamps full on.

How long more do you think it'll be before the funeral gets in? Doran asks.

Oh, I don't know, due in any minute now; but then again, these things always run late, don't they? says Long Bob.

That fellow, Patsy Doran, gives me the creeps. And no wonder, with what has been happening around here in the last while.

* * *

Vronnie Byrne is after stepping up there on to the far end of the footpath on the street. Hey, clear the way, lads, here she is; and no sneering now either, not till she passes. The thing about her – aren't there so many things about old Vronnie – she's so bent over, she looks like a tradesman's square when she's walking. She'd want to be sitting down for the top half of her body to be straight upwards facing you. When you're talking to her, she has to tilt her head sideways to look up at you with those big round searching eyes of hers – like the eyes in an oil painting that follow you around the room – and they appear so totally out of place there with the rest of her body.

Yes, here she comes now streaming along: head first, arms stretched back along by her sides and the long bony fingers crooked up to the sky, like the claws on a bat. All the men stand in by the wall, or step off the path altogether, to give her a good wide berth as she passes.

Another thing about Vronnie: she knows absolutely everything that goes on in the place. Every fit fart that happens, each scrap of information that ever was about anybody, she has it in there all stored up, ready and waiting. Her lower lip slides down off the outside of her upper lip, her mouth opens wide and her eyes bulge and flicker when she gets something new on you. She's like some exotic red and green species of bird gawping out from the cover of *National Geographic* – Master Mooney brings bundles of them to school, and gets us to cut out the pictures for sticking on the wall when an inspector is due. And boy, will Vronnie slap it up in your kisser then, the next time she sees you – but not before she's told half the country.

Vronnie can't help it though. It's just her nature to fatten off gossip and dole it out to everyone she meets. And she's not beyond capable of doing a spot of exaggerating, or spreading a few lies, about anyone who crosses her or she doesn't happen to like. There's many a brave fellow as starts to get queer fidgety when that one's shape appears over the horizon.

I see Red Bill has his hand up to his mouth as Vronnie passes. He leans over to Patsy Doran beside him and is about to say something, but waits till she's gone a few feet past hearing. It must be something worthwhile – coming from Bill.

That'll be some crooked tree they'll cut down when old Vronnie kicks the bucket, he says in a low voice.

Why's that? says Doran.

To make a crooked box for her, of course. Keeping a straight face, Bill asks: Tell me, and you being a smarter man nor me any day of the week, would you be able to fit her into an ordinary straight coffin? When you'd lay her head back, her legs would fly up in the air; push down her legs and her head would pop up, looking at you face on.

The men nearby try to hold back the guffaws. Can you imagine then the problem for the poor old priest? says Bill, cocking out the chest as he swaggers out on to the middle of the path, pouting his lips and with his thumbs stuck in under his gallowses, mimicking Father Breen. He'd have to write one of them great episcopal letters to the bishop, says he, as he spits on the road for effect.

My dear eminent bishop, we have a *dialimma* here: what are we to do with her? How will we bury her? Will it be feet up, or sitting up? Please reply by return of post, as she is starting to *dicay*.

Patsy Doran faces into the wall, hiding the snigger.

Oh, you better watch yourselves now, you smart bastards. Vronnie has better hearing nor you might think she has. But not showing any sign of hearing or heeding them, she walks along in her freshly washed wellingtons, right on up to the end of the path, then stops and gives a good look around. She takes a right turn in through the church gate, and on to where the black crones stand as rigid as statues: for once not even talking, only waiting before they go into the church.

Long Bob, who can see over most people's heads, shouts: Here it is. Mrs Brennan kicks her way along the pebblestone path, appears through the gap in the high hedge and goes up to the church gable.

Clang! Silence comes down on the place again and settles around the churchyard, where the black spider women at last begin to disappear into the dark of the church. There's an extra stir outside on the street. The men along the path move out from the wall and fix their heads in the same direction.

Another clang: the second in the toll. And again, the silence settles. A long black motor appears around the bend in the road at the far end of the village, moving along at a crawl pace. A crowd is walking behind. All the men on the path, and the people standing across the street opposite the church gate, stop talking and go back into themselves; like hens going into the safety of their coop at nightfall to roost and shelter from foxes and things of the dark.

Clang! The engine under the bonnet chugs on, as the big black Dodge goes right up to the silvery gates of the churchyard and comes to a halt. The claps of the leather footsteps on the street behind the hearse linger on for just those few seconds longer. The air in the place is gone so still and heavy.

The poor little innocent waif; anyway, an awful thing to happen to a youngster, says Long Bob.

What do you mean *waif*? I shout.

A dreadful tragedy, says he.

An awful tragedy; the family's to be pitied really, another fellow says back to him.

A terrible thing altogether happening like that, a terrible thing, Long Bob says.

What are they going on for with this old raumaish? Ah, for feck sake, Bob, speak to me; or, as big as you are, I'll clock you if you don't give over with that talk. This is me here; I'm no fucking waif, whatever that is, and I'm not to be pitied either. Do you understand? I don't want your shagging pity, and I'm no more an innocent than you are, you miserable big hoor. Why didn't you stay at home, if all you're going to do is talk about me like this?

Ah, what's the use. He can neither hear nor see me. Kicking him in the shins is no good either. There's no point hanging around these lads, listening to such black talk. It's so blasted empty. Everything is so shagging empty and dark . . . And the time between the single strokes is getting shorter.

Clang! The two hackney cars, carrying the family, have already stopped behind the hearse. A back door of the first car opens. Aidan gets out, walks around and opens the other back door. Ciss gets out. Aidan stands helping my mother shuffle her way off the back seat and climb out on to the street.

I want to see her eyes, but I can't, for her head is lowered. I want to catch her by the hand, like when I was little and we'd go off together visiting my aunt's – her sister – after dinner of a Sunday. I want to make her hear me, take away the trouble from her face and set everything right, like it must have been long ago, when there was only the two of them and Aidan. But I can do nothing.

Nearly like that evening way back; I was around seven or eight at the time. Me and little Ciss came home from school, and Mam wasn't there. When I didn't find her in the house – she'd generally be inside at that time of the evening when we'd get home – I went out around the yard looking for her. Up into the haggard – the small field beside the yard where

the hayshed and ricks of straw are – and in around
the shed, I'd go; then check up and down the road
outside. No sign of her anywhere.

It was some sight, boy, when she arrived back in
later on. Totally different she was: her mouth and
gums were all bulged out, fat. She must have found
the look on my face funny, for she started to
laugh. But soon as she opened her mouth there was
nothing but teeth, top and bottom. Big white new
teeth where I'd never seen teeth before, except for
the one or two old fag-stained fangs sticking out
like leaning fence posts she'd had taken out months
before. Lord, Mam, what's after happening to you?
says I. She leaned forward, slapping her knees and
bursting her sides, laughing at me with those new
teeth of hers. She was talking funny as well. Sort
of hissing her words out, like Humphrey Bogart
lisping in the pictures below at the hall. It was a queer
thing.

That new woman wasn't the mother I knew; it was
real suspicious or something. Maybe we had one of
those changelings in the house, a swapped mother, a
queer old harpy there in her place trying to be my real
mother. The shock and suspicion together was too
much to handle; I ran like blazes out of the house.

And all she could do was laugh. It took me ages to get used to her then.

Here now, it's hard to believe she's the same woman, she's bloody aged so much. Ah, and there goes all that black again: hat, coat, shoes and stockings. I wish she'd worn her woolly fawn coat; she always looked so snappy in that. Mam always loved the bright colours.

The people from the next car, little Jimmy and the two aunts, have already made their way out on to the street and are standing just behind the hearse. One of the aunts has her arm round Jimmy's shoulder, leaning him into her side. And they're dressed in black. Does nobody have anything to wear any more except black?

Back to the first car again. The front passenger door opens slowly, like as if it didn't want to open. Out gets – oh now wait for it, yes, now we're ready – the main man. Introducing the great lord and master, that big chief boss-man, almighty leader himself, one and only . . . rapatatap . . . the old fellow. Where is the brass band? Ra ra diddle a ra ra. Bum bum. Ra ra diddle a ra ra.

And why must he be here, can anyone tell me? Why was he invited? After all, this is my show isn't it, my show for once? So I should have some say in this little matter of who attends and who arrives in bloody hackney cars, shouldn't I?

There are people I want at my funeral and people I don't want. Not many that I don't want, mind you, but he is one of them. Definitely not on the list. No special invitation for him. Why should anyone want their blasted enemy around at a time like this? No, no. He is out – kaput, finito – as far as I'm concerned. That bastard.

2

IN THE BEGINNING WE WEREN'T ENEMIES, STARING EACH other down across the battle line. It wasn't always a duel to the death between him and me. I can remember away back to the early days, to a time when I actually called him Dad. You could say we got on not too badly at all then. Was only in the last few years, I suppose, that things really went to the dogs.

One of my earliest memories – kind of half-dream, half-memory – was of him picking me up in his arms one night I was scared of the thunder. Used to be afraid of my life in the thunder. I'd run under the table, stick my fingers in my ears and close my eyes, for the smallest rumble even. When he spotted me huddled up there under the table, he reached down and picked me up in his big vice-grip hands. It felt safe in his arms. He stayed patiently with me for hours till the clattering and flashing passed over. After that, when there was thunder at night, we'd sit together and he'd count between the flashes and the claps, till I became fairly nifty at telling whether the lightning was near or not. Wasn't so afraid of the thunder ever after. He was a different man then. And it was a different world.

I remember another time. We were walking along the headland of a ploughed field one spring, and he was telling me the names of wild flowers, trees and about how God made all the things. There was a certain feel about it – one of those good-to-be-alive sort of moments – listening to him. He took his time and picked the right way to put things simply for me. Not that I knew then much of what he was on about, but what he said stayed with me and, when I remembered it a few years later, I was able to make sense of it.

I used to sit up on the back of the Massey Ferguson, the toolbox on the mudguard for a seat, when he'd go out ploughing. The shiny steel plough, buried deep, would go on for ever turning over those lines of sods, two at a time. But it didn't matter. Nothing mattered, you'd get so mesmerized. Everything else was forgotten when you were out there in the wide open fields. You were sort of lost beyond yourself, while becoming part of the tractor, the plough and the long furrows; edges of furrows like the edge of a knife, boy. Mad gulls went squawking, high-stepping it and hopping around off the brown sods behind the plough and pecking at one another over earthworms. It was like being on another planet.

That was all before the job of ploughing and tilling was handed over to Aidan, when he finished off going to the Tech in town and became a big man all of a sudden, at about fifteen.

Whenever I was with the old man on my own doing things, or he taking his time explaining everything, me and him could be very much on the same track. Back then: lifelong butties, you might say, with no Aidan around knowing it all or little Ciss to butt in, always asking questions. I didn't see things in any other way. I was as important to him as the sunshine is to summer, as dark is to night, and I felt it without actually knowing it was so. Those times are still in the back of my head someplace, but I don't want to think about them. Too many other things have happened since.

It wasn't until I was five or six – sometime after little Jimmy was born – that I started having my doubts about the old man, and began to see him as a bit of a queer coon.

I was waiting on the steps outside the dairy door one day for Mam to come out of the kitchen with a kettle of boiling water, to help her with the churning. Mam was a dab hand at the churning. She could turn the handle of that old barrel all day long and not a bother on her. In with the boiling water, on with the lid, tighten the hinges and away with her like billy-o. When she'd have it warmed up after the first few slow, tough turns, let out all the gas and got a rhythm going, that's when she'd start up the singing.

Let him go, let him tarry, let him sink or let him swim.
He doesn't care for me, and I don't care for him . . .

The soured cream slurped and slushed evenly inside to the beat of the song. Round and round and up and down, her bib-covered body would go swinging along after the iron handle, bursting that churning out of it. Stop, she'd shout any time I'd go stomping in the puddles of water left lying here and there on the dairy floor after she had scalded the churn. Stop splashing the place, like a good lad. I had to be doing something and it was nice seeing the diamond drops sparkle, for an instant, through the shafts of brightness that raked in from the lead quarry window.

I was mainly hanging around for a slug of fresh buttermilk afterwards. Me and Aidan: the only ones in the house keen on the buttermilk. Aidan, boy, would go to town on the stuff altogether.

I went into the dairy, betimes, to find Aidan with his face stuck down in a bowl of buttermilk. He'd rub it into his ears, round the neck and all, then pat it softly over his nose and cheeks. Like your one, Mrs Rourke below of the hill, puffing the powder on her cocked bony face, before she'd law-de-daw it up to Mass, off into town or anywhere else. Aidan would have this mighty white face on him, two big eyes grinning out and the drops of buttermilk hanging off his eyebrows. Some picture he was then. What do you want to be doing that for? says I.

He was fed up, I suppose, of telling me to mind my own business, or maybe he forgot to. Instead he said: Ah, Mam says it's healthy for the skin, specially good for the complexion. Some notion of himself!

He had to have the face right, the complexion shipshape, seeing as he was after that Minnie Brien one from the street above. The one with the skinny legs and tight arse on her. I'd say Aidan would have jumped into the churn and lived in the butter if it would've improved his chances with that one. No accounting for taste, is there?

Anyway, I was still too small for lending much of a hand at the churning. I didn't mind giving the odd few turns, though; that wasn't too hard. Besides, Mam and her singing did all the drudgery; only asking me to give it a go when she wanted a break to light a fag.

Churning day used to come around about once a fortnight, when the cream vat was full and well soured. And that day had landed. Mam was due out any minute with the kettle of water, the usual, like.

Only didn't this great roaring and screaming start up inside in the house. The next thing Mam came out the front door and marched straight up the yard towards the gate. My father came flying out after her, grabbed an old galvanized bucket from outside the porch and darted across to the dung-lough outside the cowhouse at the bottom of the yard. He scraped up some of the rotten cow-piss slop into the bucket, then chased up the yard after Mam. The whole thing was a farce. It was like they were having fun.

When she took to running, he let fly with the slop from the bucket. More than anything in the world, I hoped he'd missed her. Go on with yourself then be damned, you old witch, he bellowed after her like a peppering bull. She shouted back, swearing at him in some half-crazy lingo I didn't understand, and put fierce curses on the day she ever agreed to marry him or have anything to do with him and his like.

This was no fun they were having. I'd never seen them in such a state. It was petrifying, and I began screaming out of me. The whole thing turned into one of those horrible nightmares, where red slushy blood would flow, mix with green slime, and together they would chase you into a corner before turning into long upward-pointing fingers and choking you till you'd wake up gasping.

I must have been roaring my head off something mighty, for the two of them stopped dead in their tracks at the top of the yard and turned to look at me. It wasn't meant, by either of them, that I should see their carry-on. Mam came running and sobbing back down the yard, put her arms round me and tried to cover my eyes with one of her hands. I put my hand up to her head and felt the wet slime sticking to her hair. So he hadn't missed. Her black, wet mane reaching down to her shoulders – it was normally tied up in a bun at the back of her head, like other women's – and that fierce stare in her eyes made her look a wild thing, a wounded hare or something. She smelled something awful too. My face was next to hers, and her salty tears were stinging my cheeks.

Himself was still rooted to the spot at the top of the yard, the bucket hanging by his side. His eyes were fixed on me, I thought. He'd called Mam a witch, and at that moment me and the witch were there together on the same steps, in cahoots. Mam was no Hallowe'en witch, I knew that, and I glared back at him.

Mam and I sat on the steps for ages. Shush . . . shush . . . Ah shush now. Shhhh . . . it'll be all right, it'll be all right, was all she said, and rocked the two of us. Eventually I said: Mam, when I'm big, I won't let him do that to you so I won't. I'll kill him and kick the shit out of him if he ever does. She stretched back her head, looked down at me with those strange, fierce eyes of hers, laughed and nodded. Some woman to laugh was Mam, and at the queerest of moments.

It wasn't until little Ciss woke up bawling, after slipping off the old couch inside – as usual – banging her head, that Mam stood up and took off with herself into the house. He was still up the yard, in the same place, fiddling at something or other. Then he started to walk down to where I was. But sitting there on my own, I got afraid of him all of a sudden and ran away into the house after Mam. That was the start of the rot, I think. I knew then that things would never be the same.

It wasn't an easy sleep that night. I kept on waking up out of these bad dreams. My bed was in the room next to theirs, right alongside the partition that kept the two rooms apart. The old sheet boards weren't much thicker than the layers of wallpaper that stuck to them, and you could hear every sound in the other room, especially if your head was up close. Whenever I did wake up that night, and many a night after, I got anxious about Mam, wondering was she all right, like. Was she safe in there with him?

Once during the night I woke up and heard him calling her, in a low voice: Annie . . . Hey, Annie, are you awake? Are you awake, Annie? Will you come on over in here to me, Annie?

After this calling lark going on and on, I could hear Mam eventually shuffle out of her bed, slap-slap across the floor and get in beside him in his big bed. The talking in low voices went on for ages. Then it stopped, and this great grunting and ahing – all muffled like – took over. His bed inside began to creak.

So they were starting to play now, were they? Wrestling, playing tig or some other game? Grown-ups – the two that I knew anyway – funny creatures, weren't they? Working all day and only playing at night in the bed, the time when the rest of us want to sleep. At least they weren't slaughtering each other any more. Mam was safe.

The gatchying went on inside for ages. That bed moved like hell, the way the old winnowing machine, the one out on the loft, would go growl and neigh like a horse, blowing the chaff off the grain way up in the heavens. The shaking would rise up through the soles of your feet, and get so bad your teeth would start to chatter. Chaff, dust and feathers rising and swirling round, all golden like, in the darts of sunlight through the loft windows. That old machine would growl on, the whole place would shake and the air choke with dust, so much that no one could stand it. Then, quicker than it'd started, the machine would slow and stop. Everything would die down and the dust settle.

There was one last groan inside in the other room,

and the bed noise stopped. All the corn was winnowed, and no more chaff was left on the grain. They had finished playing, had they? Mam slap-slapped her way back to her own caboose in the dark and, at last, I was free to let my eyes close and go to sleep.

The next Wednesday night, according to Aidan, Mam was to go to the pictures above in the hall: herself and the old lad. Ah, they were back colloguing, all palsy-walsy again. I noticed, though, Mam was a lot quieter in herself; hardly sang one song the whole week.

For ages before, I'd been plaguing herself, and then Aidan, to take me to the pictures. Every chance I had, I'd ask Aidan about the pictures, what was the hall like inside, how big was it, what colour was it, were the pictures big and will you take me with you the next night? Aidan, after telling me not once but forty times – that's what he reckoned anyway – eventually said to shut up and leave him alone. Mam said she would take me, for the bit of peace. Like the way she played tig in the bed with the old lad, I suppose: for the bit of peace as well? Even though you're far too young, says she.

Ah Mam! I never saw the pictures before and Aidan is allowed to go Wednesday night and Sunday night, says I.

Look, Tony, says she, starting to lose the rag. Aidan is a queer lot older than you, and anyway didn't I say I'd bring you. No more about it, that's that; now give my head peace.

And there was no more about it, least not out loud. What was the use of brocking on people, making a nuisance of yourself or taking away their precious bit of peace, no. But inside the head it was different. I couldn't wait for Wednesday night to arrive. Of course, what I hadn't allowed for was that when Mam said she'd bring me, she'd forgotten to say next Wednesday night.

Come on, says the old lad to Mam, it's time to go. He went out to the porch, yanking up his light gaberdine overcoat on to his shoulders. Mam was ready long before: sitting, knees together and feet apart, on the bockety arm of the couch, and wearing her wool fawn coat, black leather gloves and dark scarf, all dainty-like, there under starter's orders, waiting. And they're off. At last. Time for me to get the skids on too. I grabbed my coat, pulled it on and made for the front door after them.

And where do you think you're going, my good man? says he.

Going to the pictures as well, says I; Mam promised she'd take me.

He put his hands on my shoulders and steered me back into the kitchen. Take that coat off right now. You can go another night.

Fallen at the first fence. I plonked my arse as far down on the couch as ever I could go, too stunned to open my gob, while they were off out the door, up the yard, on to the road and gone. But the dream of seeing the pictures was like a magnet; so back up on my horse, on with the coat again, and out after them like a shot. They were well down the road before I caught up with them.

What's this carry-on here? says the old lad.

I want to go to the hall. I want to see the pictures, I yelped.

Ah, another night, Tony son, says Mam gently.

He gave me a right ringer across the puss. Go home and do what you're told, he roared, and him and her walked off in the dark. I was stinging like hell both inside and out, and felt like a right jackass into the bargain.

But when I got back to the kitchen, into the brightness, Aidan was in the middle of the floor. He was in a fit tearing round an upside-down twig, the handle stuck down into the middle of the coal bucket and Luxembourg blasting the house out of it:

> *If there's annathin that ya want*
> *If there's annathin I can do uh hu*
> *Just call on me, an I'll send it along*
> *With loove from me to youuu.*

He was wound up. The speed of him: a swirl round, a step and swirl again, his head ducking in under his arm, which was stretched out holding on to the ends of the twig bristles. He went Gaa de boum chou, filling up the break in the song. *Just call on me, an I'll send it along*, and a real quick Gaa de boum chou before *With loove from me to youuu* . . . and a Gaa de boum chou. Gaa de boum chou. *I gut orms that loong ta hold you / And keep you by moi soide* . . . Gaa de boum chou.

Lashing into it he was, there on the cement floor. Himself and the brush – the little beaut; thin, straight and tight-arsed, just like Minnie Brien. That's the way he liked 'em; nothing could be done for him. We had the house all to ourselves; the wireless on full belt,

Aidan flailing like a loony and me and Ciss sitting stitching our sides at him. We watched Aidan awhile, then jumped up and tried to ape him. We joined in: *If there's annathin that ya want . . .*

A mighty spell had fallen on the place. Some magician had passed that way and changed everything, freed us of grown-ups, orders and stuff, then decided to light up our house: one speck of light there in all the dark of night in the world. There was a new wildness to this freedom, and along with the music the whole thing filled the kitchen to bursting point nearly. Mad and wild: mighty. And it belonged to us. Though, at the same time, you knew it was all going to end in a moment or two with the end of the song. The music ground down and faded off. But laa datdat datdat daa . . . kept on going inside my head despite the crackling from the wireless.

I wanted to let none of it go, or nothing to change. But no matter how I tried, both the words and the air faded. The spell was over, the magic gone. The only thing left was static.

3

EVENTUALLY, I GOT TO THE PICTURES. ME AND AIDAN AND Mam together. We went into the hall and sat down facing a white sheet that hung in front of these long wine-red curtains.

Strange: all the gawks in the place were staring at nothing on the white sheet, instead of turning round the other way, where there was at least something to watch. This machine thing, like the separator in the dairy at home, sat high up on a stand at the back of the hall, and Long Johnny Codd was perched up there on a ladder alongside looking into it, fixing it or something. Long Johnny, the separator man.

Why was everyone's back turned on Johnny and his great machine? I went about turning my carcass on the stool, to face the right way around where the picture was. If nobody else was going to look at you, Johnny boy, I might as well, seeing as there wasn't much else doing round there. Pictures me arse, I says, what was all the fuss for anyway? Aidan reached across Mam and gave me a belt on the back of the head.

Stop, says Mam, you're making a show of me, the two of you.

Then the lights went out, Long Johnny and his separator were lost in the dark, with nothing but this great shaft of brightness. Some girl's voice screamed out: Keep your dirty big hands to yourself. There was a spate of laughing. I turned myself back around on the stool. There we were, facing all these crosses flashing on the white sheet hanging in front of us, and no end of writing. Till at last men appeared: mighty black and white fellows in hats and waistcoats, all shooting the shite out of each other, loud as anything. Ah yah! So this was the stuff! Now I knew what all the fuss was about. Why hadn't anyone told me before?

Away we went, boy, all on our horses across fields, jumping over rocks, going like blazes with your man in the white rigout, a black mask over his eyes. His buttie in the ponytail, a band round his forehead, rode right behind him. Imagine that, a man wearing a ponytail – hadn't yet discovered the Indians. But fair play to him all the same, ponytail or no ponytail, he was nearly as good a cowboy as the other fellow in the mask. The music blazed out to the beat of the horses' hooves: *giddyap giddyap giddyap giddyap geeedeee yap*.

The next minute the sound went muffled, gurgled, as if you'd put your fingers in your ears or stuck your head in a basin of water, and the blooming picture went all fuzzy. Lads behind started whistling and shouting. The lights were switched back on, and the racket died down. If yous don't shut up, I won't fix the shagging thing, then yous may go home, roared Long Johnny. There was another short burst of whistling and heh-hehing.

That's not a separator, you fool, that's a projector, says Aidan to me. Oh yah? Aidan should know; he knows it all. It took Johnny a couple of minutes to get her rolling again, but roll she did. Some smartass shouted: Heh, Johnny boy, get your trousers down and ride the fecking range. But that only got one or two laughs; everyone else was busy watching the cowboys starting up again. The Wild West was there in a big way, no doubt in the wide earthly world about it. Heh heh, ya boy ya, giddyap. *Giddyap giddyap giddyap giddyap geeedeee yap . . .*

Aidan was gone too big and cocked up though to bother his head playing Cowboys and Indians any more. He'd sooner play with the little squaws above in the street, says Mam at dinnertime, trying to rise him. Isn't that right, Aidan? His face reddened like a turkey cock. The problems I had trying to get somebody – anybody – to play Cowboys and Indians and have a shoot-out. The pictures had got me going. The Cowboys was the only thing for me, even though nobody else wanted to know. Then I discovered little Ciss was interested. What a find she turned out to be.

Ciss had the ponytail and all, going plink plonk from side to side like the wag of a clock, as she sat up on the wheel of the old spring-cart. She was an amazing Tonto, especially for a girl. Two years younger than me and all she was, but she sure had what it takes. You couldn't tell her that though; she might get too cocky, lose interest and feck off with herself. Mean, ugly as hell and could giddyap all day long, so she could. No matching her either for the big shoot-outs: cuish . . . cuish . . . cuishing away, real loud, like. She knew exactly how to fall down dead when she was supposed to, and there was no bawling every time she fell or got pushed. What I liked best, though, about Ciss playing was that she wasn't greedy and didn't want to be the sheriff all the time; she never minded being a robber, a bank bandit or anything like that.

Those haven't-shaved-for-months bad guys, who rode into town from out the prairie, sure had plenty of cover in summer and autumn: a shed full of hay and straw. In late winter and spring, with the fodder getting used up, there wasn't as much trouble – and not as much fun either – flushing them out. Those mean, ugly guys in swinging noisy saloons, and bad-assed bandits who hung around street corners like curs all day, were only gunning for trouble as they waited for the Central Bank to open so they could rob it.

The haggard was the whole Wild West Frontier to us. The hayshed was our town, and the spring-cart, shoved in years earlier under the lean-to at the back, we used as our headquarters, the jail, our sheriff's office, everything and anything. We sat on either side of it: high up in our saddles, with Mam's old hats on, riding the range and crossing badlands. Cuish . . . cuish . . . cuishing away. Me the Lone Ranger, Ciss Tonto. *Kemosabe*, boy.

Mogue Doyle

*   *   *

When I asked him, Mikey Doyle said he was five and a half. Had my doubts about him, though. The way he said half – hey-af, like a Waterford man – with his nose puckered up, the day he wandered up to the shed where we were on a shoot-out with Indians. His knuckles bulged out, stuck down the pockets of his short pants. What are yous doing at all? says he, whining out the *at all* bit on the end. He talked like an old man chewing tobacco. What class of maneen had we there on our hands? I almost expected to see a slimy tobacco spit, a mile long, shoot out of his mouth any second.

I'd often seen him around, but he was always hanging out of either his mother or father, and had never come near enough to get talking to. We'd only ever stared each other down from a safe distance. This time, face to face, it was a different kettle of fish: no mama's apron for him to run his head up under when I'd stick out my tongue at him. We stood like two gunslingers ready to draw any second and have it out to the bitter end. Yep, that's the way things were done in the Wild West: shoot first, talk later. It was my territory and I'd ask the questions; sure as hell wasn't going to be answering any.

He'd come over with his father who was inside in the house talking work stuff to the old lad. Ah come on, Tony, let him play, says Ciss. Will you please? I hadn't the heart to refuse. Besides, it was a way out of the showdown that was about to happen: neither of us would lose face. I was grateful for Ciss asking to let him join in.

Come on, get down. You'll have to take cover here under the rocks if you want to play, says I, bossing him. Mikey crept into the hay beside us. His face was as white as milk. Ciss put her hand up to his head and tried to straighten out one of his black curls. Where'd you get the hair like that? says she, taking a shine to him straight away. With three of us in it, them blasted Indians wouldn't stand a chance; we'd scalp them in double-quick time. We were in a posse when Mikey's father called him to go home. Me and Mikey had become right butties.

We took turns after that, going over to each other's houses, and off poking about in each other's sheds, barns and cowhouses. We'd edge round corners and dark hiding places, in case of outlaws' ambushes.

One day his mother caught us sneaking up the stone steps outside their loft. As bad now, the pair of yous, as old Vronnie Byrne for creeping around with your noses stuck in everything, says she. I didn't like the sore tongue of her, and made a face behind her back. Mikey looked at me, but said nothing.

I can see now, though, it wasn't Mikey at all who bothered her, even though she was saying it about the two of us. It was me running around, poking my nose in their business, that annoyed her. Anyway, there was very little left in either of our yards, barns, lofts or houses that we hadn't rummaged through.

Ciss would tag along most of the time, doing her best to keep up with us. I think she did it mainly so she could be around Mikey. Everything was going grand really – until the accident happened in our shed.

There was a shelf of hay cut down to within a few feet of the ground, just the right height for us to leap around on. We were in the middle of an ambush, and Mikey jumped off the shelf on to some loose hay on the ground under. None of us saw the cursed hay-knife. Razor sharp that blasted thing; had to be or it wouldn't slice through hay, and cows wouldn't get fed. The blood was only pumping out of Mikey's leg, boy, as he rolled off the loose hay and on to the ground. I think his face turned whiter than it already was, and that's saying something. He was way too shook up in himself even to open his mouth and roar.

Me and Ciss went shouting into the house to call Mam. I think Ciss thought Mikey was dead. Mam and Aidan carried him inside and put him on the couch. Some fair-sized cut he had, boy. Mam washed and dabbed it with cotton wool and iodine; he didn't even roar over that. The nurse landed and stitched him up; then wound these great bandages up and down his leg. Mikey never opened his mouth the whole time. His eyes kept rolling around, like they were attached to a swivel and operated from the back of his head.

His father came and carried him home, saying: Ah sure, it could have been worse – could have got him in the stomach. Will I leave him here with yous, missus? We have enough childer at home. You'd feel for Mikey: cut up like that, while his old fellow made little of him, offering to give him away. I was wondering would that narky old mother of his tear into Mikey the minute she'd get him home. Scrawb the fecking eyes out of you, boy, that one would. I hoped she wasn't going to come gunning for me because of it. There'd be no more playing or gallivanting about in Mikey for ages to come. He'd have to tie up his horse for a while.

Later when the old lad heard what'd happened, he turned frigging turk altogether. You could almost see the blood pumping to his face, the veins rising out through the neck. Blamed me, he did. Caught me up on his knees and bate the arse off me with the palm of his hand. But being blamed in the wrong was worse than any beating: it hurt more. What he blamed me for, or so he said, was climbing on the hay; that if it hadn't been for me, Mikey wouldn't have been up there in the first place. Didn't I tell you often enough, says he, not to be mucking up with your boots what the cattle and cows have to feed on? And what will I say to Mrs Doyle the next time I meet her?

How was I supposed to know what he'd say to her? Was I expected to forget the beating, the sore arse and all, and give a shite about what he might say to Mrs bloody Doyle – that old rip?

It was all Aidan's fault. He was the one who'd left the hay-knife thrown there. Once or twice I'd just missed it myself by a hair's breadth when I was jumping around. Never stuck it back, the way he was supposed to, in the face of the next ridge, up out of harm's way, when he'd finished cutting down fodder.

Aidan, that yoke! He couldn't have cared less: just burst in, got the job done and threw everything down after him. Then swore blind he'd put the knife back properly after the last time he'd used it. The old lad, though, would always believe him before me.

Right after I'd got the works, Mam came in from milking. When she saw me whimpering there in a corner of the kitchen, she blew her top and tore into him. What did you do to that child? says she. Blaming him for that young fellow cutting himself, aren't you? How dare you come in here and treat the boy like that. You've a bad dirty temper you have, you know that? She couldn't be stopped: You'll do damage to him some day if you're not careful.

Good on you, Mam, says I in my own mind; but don't overdo it. Can't you see his big neck starting to tighten up again, and his teeth stripping like a dog after sheep? There was going to be holy bloody war; time to take myself to hell out that kitchen.

That cursed dog-fighting between them, you just wouldn't want to be within a hundred miles of it. And after all that, they'd be sure to go playing in his big bed the same night, as if nothing had ever happened. Only another blasted nightmarish sleep for me to look forward to.

Where are you going sneaking off to like that? he roared after me. But I was already out the door and gone, letting on not to've heard him. He had his hands full dealing with Mam and wasn't going to come after me.

All that bother wouldn't put you in much humour for playing Cowboys and Indians. On my way past her, I gave Ciss a quick shift: herself and her notions of a posse-chase round the haggard. *Kemosabe* my arse. I wanted to be alone with myself, and not have to listen to the sound of any other voice. Sick to the teeth of voices, I was. People were getting to be a real pain in the neck. I needed to get rid of the shouting and ringing going on in my ears.

There at the top of the haggard under the drooped branches of an evergreen tree – one of the ones the old grandfather was supposed to have brought back with him from America – right in the middle of the briars and bushes that were never cut, nobody would know where to find you; no one ever came. The way it should be. No matter how well you might get on with someone or how much you'd share other hides and things with them, a spot like that was never shared. It was your secret place for getting away from people. How long though, I wondered, before Ciss would cop on to it, and need to go there, too, to be on her own. Maybe she'd find someplace else. I hoped she would.

A cat or dog might drop in the odd time. Sniffing its nose along under the branches, it would suddenly stop, lift its head, eyes wide from the start of seeing you, then jump back and off with it again. You'd have the place all to yourself once more. There were always a few birds around – not that you'd mind them; especially that one robin. At least I thought it was the same one all the time. Real cheeky, too: tail pointed towards you while watching you sideways with the one eye. The very same way as old Vronnie Byrne used to do.

And who's to say it wasn't Vronnie; that she wasn't the robin hopping around, watching what was going on? Maybe that's why she was so bent over: to perch on branches the way birds do and not fall off. That could've been it. For didn't everyone say that nothing happened that Vronnie didn't know about? I hadn't a clue, though, what she did with them wellingtons when she was off flying and bobbing about; didn't see the robin wearing them. There was a queer one for you: Vronnie changing into a bird to get a better view of what went on.

A right one for Aidan. I'd have to tell him to mind himself going into the dairy; make sure to close the door before pasting his face with buttermilk. It wouldn't do at all if that ever got out. Hey, Aidan, how's it going there? Did you happen to notice the robin outside the dairy door? Can never be too careful now. With Vronnie going up to the street so often lately, you know, certain scrawny-arsed girls might get wind of what goes on with bowls of buttermilk inside a certain dairy. That wouldn't do at all. They might only fall around the street laughing. Now, Aidan, don't say you weren't warned; that's how these things get out. It's the queer times we're living in.

After sitting there in the shade for ages, propped against the butt of the tree, it was coming back to me what Mam had said to the old lad: her warning him about his bad temper and doing damage. She was dead right: he did have one hoor of a temper. And whenever anything went wrong, or luck ran against him, he went berserk. Once, I saw him tightening up the arm of a plough behind the tractor; the next thing the spanner slipped – fhuuuu. He skelped the knuckles off an iron bar underneath, bits of skin came away and blood dripped from his fingers. The curses of him, boy. The next moment the old spanner went flying at the first thing he saw. It hit the glass cover of the road-tax disc holder on the tractor, smashing it to pieces, sending bits of glass flying. Imagine someone's head there instead of the disc holder! Not that it would've made much difference to him what it was.

No bother to him to give a bullock a right good kick: some fat bucko lying in the way when he'd want to feed cattle in a hurry in the evenings. Because the poor beast would be slow to move from the doorway, he'd end up getting his nuts kicked in; immediately his back would hunch up from the pain. The man was pure dangerous to be around when he was like that.

There, between the green fronds on the end of a branch, I could see out across the haggard in a straight line: right through the gate opening below, down to the bottom of the yard. Mam, a white enamel bucket in her hand, was legging it over to the draw-well for water.

She went around the far side of the well and turned the handle – slowly at first – letting the rope off the wooden roller and the bucket drop down the well. The big iron wheel, on this end of the roller, picked up speed and started to spin; she let it spin – not too fast – of its own accord, as she'd normally do. The wheel came to a sudden stop: the bucket had reached the water and Mam had grabbed the handle, not letting off any more rope. A couple of seconds for the bucket to fill, and the wheel started to grind round the opposite way. She turned it with the same ease as she turned the handle of the churn.

The axle badly needed oil: it squeaked like hell with each slow turn, right the way to the top. The wire rope wound around the pulley block again, hauling the full bucket up out of the hole and into the full light of day. Mam opened the half-door and pulled out the galvanized bucket, battered as could be from clattering down off the sides of the well. After emptying the water into the enamel house bucket, alongside on the ground, she closed the draw-well door behind her. Her free arm reached out swinging and pointing – she leaned sideways for balance – as she hecked her way back to the house, dragging the full bucket down off the calf of her right leg.

Hold on, Mam, will you for feck sake, till I get down there and give you a hand. I had my mouth open to shout at her, but there was something stopping me, keeping me from getting it out. A sort of voice in my head said not to make a sound or stir from my place against the butt of the tree. It wasn't safe to go out.

I wanted to curl up inside myself like a hedgehog in the grass; stay there for evermore, with no one to bother me, only the odd stray dog or cat and the robin hopping around. Yah, old Vronnie the robin, she'd talk to me and let me know everything that was happening outside, and I'd be snug there always under the tree in the soft light. I caught a last glimpse of Mam dragging the bucket out of sight behind the pier of the gate. Then she was gone.

All of a sudden I got this horrible dread of the draw-well, and for no reason. I had this odd notion that the draw-well was alive, a monster right there in our own yard. A frightening, cursed thing you'd never want to go near. Then it came to me: the time Mam, when I'd been much smaller, had brought me with her for water. She'd lifted me up so I could look in over the half-door. I saw right down into the shaft: black and green stone walls and small fronds of sickly green fern growing outwards. Far down in the darkness, the water, smooth as glass, had a dead sheen to it.

I hadn't been afraid at all then. Mam'd held on to me so tightly anyway, it nearly kept me from swallowing my breath. She said that that was where the cold water we drank came from, to look how deep down it was; and I was never, ever, to go near it or open the door no matter what. That if I did, I'd fall in and that would be the end of me for all time; I'd never be seen or heard tell of again. What she had tried to do was frighten the shite in me, so I'd stay away and not even play within an ass's roar of the spot. But the fear thing hadn't taken hold there and then. I didn't know much about fear, or maybe I was afraid of a different sort of thing. She was the one who'd been terrified; clasping me for dear life the way she did, in case she'd let slip.

It wasn't until I was there under the tree, having seen Mam at the well, that the fear, after all that time, started to grow. It grew and clasped at my insides like a vice-grip. Kind of how it is with, say, corn seed. It lies there in the earth, asleep for weeks; then one day it wakes up all of a sudden, and bursts out of the ground in one mad rush for the sky. Just like that, the fear must have been asleep. But the bad bastard had woken up and was gripping tight, making up for lost time.

Not that I was afraid for myself. No reason to be: I didn't go near the draw-well. Not much use in sending me for water. I couldn't carry a bucket without spilling it all, and I wasn't strong enough to wind the bucket up the well. What was scary was watching Mam going over to open that door, lest something awful might happen. She could lose her balance, slip on the wet ground and fall in. What then? The worst part was when, with the door open, she'd reach in to grab and pull out the full bucket. At that point, I couldn't help but look away. The fear would ease again when she'd close the door after her: only then was she safe. I was glad that Aidan did most of the going for water.

The funny thing about Aidan: as heedless as he was doing chores, when he went for water he was much more careful than Mam. He'd make sure to keep the door closed till the last minute, stand well back from the edge, and hold on to the rail with one hand as he'd reach in for the bucket with the other. Amazing how exact he was — except, that is, starting it off. He always gave the iron handle a quick jerk, a swing and then let it go spinning like bedamned. The old galvanized bucket would clatter down the well, knocking off the sides, making a fierce racket you'd hear a mile away. And you'd say: Ah, there's Aidan going for the water.

The round, iron roof made the well look like one of those small round-capped perfume boxes you'd see in the chemist's window in town at Christmas. Except this box had a half-door in the front. The roof curved down over the front of the wooden roller inside. Anyone getting water had to look out for cats and things, perched inside on top of the roller, before they turned the handle. A hen or chicken might fall in, the odd cat even.

It was always Aidan's fault: he was the one who jerked the handle round without bothering his arse to look in and check. Some stir that caused around the place. Fellows tied ropes to buckets, bits of wire mesh and iron grappling hooks – I had not known what they were for. They lit up John Players, in between trying to fish out the dead cat. It took ages to get a grip and pull the animal into the bucket below. Then up she flew and was thrown on the ground, flat as a pancake, soggy wet. I kept on watching that cat lying stretched, drying out, like she was sleeping in the sun. I waited for her to waken, jump up and run away.

Then someone would hint to Aidan that he'd done

it. Oh, will you go 'way will you? says he, real indignant that they should dare blame him. Of course I checked; what do you take me for, a fool? There was definitely no cat there the last time I got water. But everyone knew the story. Saying no more, they just looked at him with that special *huh* smile.

Some time later, another cat went in. A stray dog chased one of our cats, a brown tabby with enormous green eyes, in the gate and down the yard. She crawled up the frame of the well, tore in over the door, balanced herself and jumped across on to the pulley. But there was too much wire rope on the pulley and not enough wood for her claws to grip and hold. She scratched and clung on for all she was worth, but there's no give to steel. The terrified animal dropped down, I heard the mewing fade away, and a far-off splash. The cat cried a while, a faint cry, then no more. And nothing could have been done about it.

Crouched up there against the butt of the tree, I was thinking about how the draw-well would take the living spark from a body. Such an easy thing to happen, but not so easy to forget: this taking of a life. A picture of the stupid cat clawing away at the pulley kept coming back to me. I was mad with her for going near the well; wanted to kick her arse up the yard to safety. But I couldn't as the thing had happened a year or more before. Nothing would change that. I was still angry and didn't know why. In my head, the cat kept on clawing away its last moments for ever: it never quite dropped down that dark cursed hole – only always on the point of – and it never passed the miserable bits of pale green fern that ought to have known better than set up shop in such a spot. No matter how hard I tried, I couldn't manage to see her actually falling, or hitting the water – the hungry, open-mouthed, black waters of death below.

The same draw-well water would turn crystal clear the minute it reached the top; the same damned two-faced water we all drank and made tea with. Hard to understand how one minute it was a killer and the next minute it cured the thirst. But death-waters were what was down there, nothing else.

Then another thing started haunting me. I could hear myself counting one, two, three, till I heard a splash. It kept going around inside my head: one, two, three . . . splash; one, two, three . . . splash. It reminded me of when the old lad used to take me on his knee and count between the flash and the bang during thunder. But this time, the fear just wouldn't go away.

I remembered, too, how the water in the draw-well couldn't be used, not even touched, for weeks afterwards. And we had to traipse off to the old spring well a couple of fields away, that only cattle drank from. The scum and flies had to be skimmed off the top, before we dipped the gallon can to fill the bucket.

Talking of cats, this huge fellow, the biggest one, I swear, I'd ever laid eyes on, came nodding in from the long grass. Sniffed its way right up under the drooped branches of the tree. The sight of that bucko brought me right back to where I was. I didn't budge an inch. Some size: more like a buck rabbit or hare, the very same fur. Aidan used to call this colour – and every other colour he couldn't put a name to – deduckety grey like a mouse's diddy. I burst out laughing. The mixture of sobbing and laughing rose through the branches. The shagging cat, all in the one go, froze up, glared at me, turned round and tore off with itself like crazy, its baggy underbelly flopping off the weeds as it ran. The big green-yellow eyes of it. Amazing how it never spotted me till the last moment. I thought cats were supposed to be sharp.

I sat there imagining what it must be like to be a

dog. To tear out after that cat, barking through the long grass down the haggard and up the stone steps to the loft, sending deduckety grey thieves of pigeons fluttering off the seed barley and out through the grill windows. I yapped like a terrier and savoured every minute of the chase – all in my head. I'd run that cat up and down till there was no place left for it to escape. There was only one spot where the creature might go that I wouldn't give chase. Or would I?

The chill was biting at my toes. I'd have to get out of my hiding place soon, and face going back into the house for heat and food, if nothing else.

4

THE HEARSE'S ENGINE IS NO SOONER SWITCHED OFF THAN who should pop out but Amby Loony Mooney. Out from the same gap in the hedge that Mrs Brennan went into a few seconds earlier: one minute it's Mrs Brennan, the next minute Loony Mooney. Is this some sort of game: now you see me, now you don't? Or, as the song says: *she stepped in and he stepped out again* . . . raadellie daadellie daadellie die.

Yes, man in a million Mooney, head bottle-washer and schoolmaster supreme, steps out there on to the gravel path, stops, looks over the street, puts a hand to the head, turns and goes back into the hedge. Then out he comes again – this is getting worse – marching in all his glory. Oh no! Oh, sweet feck, wait for it.

Will you look who's coming out behind him, and marching too, if you don't mind? It's the yobs from fifth and sixth classes.

> *Oh, come down from the mountain, Katie Daly,*
> *Come down from the mountain, Katie, do . . .*

Kicking and darting the pebbles off the gravel path: you'd think it was hailstones beating off the windscreen of Patsy Doran's car. Hop to it now, my old flowers, one, two – keep in line there – one, two, and a one, two. Let there be no streeling now either. I hope you're all here; don't want no one missing, staying at home not bothering their arse to come. Hey Master Mooney, did you call the roll? What! *Anseo* for everybody; right so, good on you, lads. Wait, though, did your man Mikey come? Don't see him.

They march out, as far as the churchyard gate, then divide up into two lots and stand on either side of the path facing each other: all done exactly right to Corporal Fidgety's orders. That's Mooney for you. Fair play to you, Master Mooney, boy; some of the girls carrying flowers, too. Well, be the hokey, man! Isn't that nice now.

Hey, what's the chance of running up behind

Jordie there and giving her big lardy arse a good pinch? Whoops! Or catch Willy Murphy by the pecker, make him give out that woeful squeal of his. How's she hanging there, Willy Pecker Murphy, boy? Hates being called Pecker, he does. Gets him going though; I love to get him going.

But, yeow uuull, will you look at Brudgie Whelan, will you? The snow-white stockings running up them long legs of hers to the knees, and then the bare soft pink flesh on the underside going up, way up under the line of the plaid skirt. Well boys, oh boys. What wouldn't I give to be standing beside her, and tickle the palm of her hand maybe, what! And say something funny to make Brudgie giggle – always great to see her like that. Not so much that tittery laugh either, as the nice smile she has before she breaks into a full giggle. Nothing in the whole world quite like it.

Anyway, there's no great laugh to that lot there now. Some queer sullen-looking shower of faces yous are. Hey lads, for feck sake, it's not a funeral yous are at! Do something. Will one of yous make them girls laugh. I'll tell you what: we'll have a bit of an old dance, anything at all. Forget Mooney and his big Mac's Smile face; throw everything else there to one side. Least for now, anyway. Let's have it, Andy boy, have you got the mouth organ in the inside pocket there with you? Miss Brudgie, may I have the pleasure of this dance, please.

Myself, to be sure, got free invitations
For all the nice girls and boys I might ask.
And just in a minute, both friends and relations
Were dancing as merry as bees round a cask.
There was lashings of punch and wine for the ladies,
Potatoes and cakes, there was bacon and tea.
There were the Nolans, the Dolans, O'Gradys
Courting the girls and dancing away.

Six long months I spent in Dublin,
Six long months doing nothing at all.
Six long months I spent in Dublin,
Learning to dance for Lanigan's Ball.

Ah, come on, yous. Hey lads, do yous remember when we were scuts way back in the old Battleaxe's class? Oh, all right, I give up. What's the fecking use anyway.

You know the stillness in this place is only blinding. Each of them stands there rigid. Side faces: a luscious pale, throwing off to one side the last of the evening light, showing up the golden brown freckles on half-washed necks and cheeks. See the tidemarks? But it doesn't matter. They're here, isn't that right? Isn't that what counts?

The light matters too. It's that peculiar rose-light this time of evening only, while the sun sits on the tit of the Blackstairs, saying goodbye, readying itself to drop off behind. The heads of hair, along the two rows, are as fresh as the spring meadows full of pot-belly cattle away on the flatlands beyond the far valley. Each head with two sides to it: the light side and the shaded – the shadows, the dark side. Why must there always be a dark side? Will you tell me that, Master Mooney? Will you tell me *as Gaeilge*: tá mar a ya mar a ye ya ya. Yah!

He's out there now at the church gate talking low to the hearse driver, showering him with spits at the rate of a mile a minute, going from one foot to the other. Gets queer excited, the man.

Anyway, back to the lads. Will yous come on. *O six long months I spent in Dublin / Six long months doing nothing at all . . .*

Don't see Mikey Doyle anywhere. Where the hell is he? Hey! Did anyone see Mikey Doyle? I'd like to get my hands on that little cunt. Did his old one bother her backside coming? No loss anyway if she didn't. Maybe herself and her little Mikey pet will want to make a grand entrance, too, like what the old lad did. They'll leave it to the last, maybe. Aw, bollocks, what does it matter?

Doesn't Brudgie look queer well, though? It'd do your heart good just to see her standing there. *Six long months I spent in Dublin* . . . Raadellie daadellie daadellie daa.

5

I'M NOT TOO SURE HOW MUCH I HAVE IN MY HEAD ABOUT the early days, or even the early years, in school. There was a September morning sun when Mam brought me that first time on the carrier of her bike. Click click click went the chain downhill, click clack clack uphill. To keep you out of the muck and try to make a good impression, Mam said, for the first day at least. Aren't you getting to be the right heavy lump now? says she, smiling, as she gawked at me with big brown sad eyes. Bare legs jangled off the carrier, splayed out over the stony road; lording it off there on the back of the bike, getting wheelied along. New sandals, corduroy trousers, the works. She said I was the real little showman the way I looked. Ah, that school lark was going to be the life; the smell of new corduroy was a great smell.

But nobody had taken the trouble to warn me, had they! Where I was really heading to was the slaughterhouse. There was this walking battleaxe of an old one inside at the blackboard just waiting to knock the shit, the showman or anything else for that matter, out of fellows like me. A holy terror she was. And the size of her!

I think even Mam was afraid of her. They spoke only a couple of words when we landed, and I was dumped there at the door. Then off went Mam on her bike, like the wheels of hell. When Mrs Doyle brought Mikey the first day, and many a day after, it was a different story. She spent ages outside in the corridor chatting and laughing away, buttering up the Battleaxe. No fear of her tearing off, leaving Mikey to the mercy of your one. Mrs Doyle would let it be known she existed all right; no better woman, one to be reckoned with.

I can see now what she was on about: letting it be known her little Mikey was only on loan to the school, like, for a few hours in the day; doing the best deal she could to pave the way for him. And who'd blame her? As for Mam: oh, I don't know. Maybe she didn't know her tables, ABCs and stuff. Afraid she'd get dragged in, made to sit down, questioned and found out to know nothing. She'd probably made the right choice so, getting to hell out of the place as fast as ever she could. Mrs Doyle wasn't afraid, though. I bet you she knew her ABCs.

The Battleaxe was some monstrous heap, boy. I saw a lad so scared of her one day, he shit his corduroys. It slithered down his purple legs and over his white ankle socks, like lava down a mountain and steam rising. It seeped into the holes of his sandals; most of it slumped in a puddle on the floorboards. The pong in the place was only heinous. The little hoor must have been eating carrion and onions or something.

The Battleaxe sent for his big brother in sixth class, and made him scrub the floor and wash down your man, who was shivering and whining away like the wind through telegraph wires, standing there in the middle of his own belongings, too small and scared to know what to do. The Battleaxe kept shouting and pounding away sums, tables and stuff, while treating the two brothers as if they didn't exist, except for the odd sideways glance and a swallowing scowl as she pursed her lips. The white stubble would bristle round her gigantic puss, and turn over like the whiskers of a Jack Russell snarling. A good shave? Shave me arse, a fecking mowing bar and tractor wouldn't do a job on that face.

The wash mark lasted for years on that floor. The stench of Jeyes Fluid fairly hung around for days, hitting you in the face every time you'd go back in the room. It wasn't till I was in fifth or sixth class myself that I got any idea of the embarrassment the older brother must have gone through: having to face his butties, the girls and all, after that. Imagine swaggering up to some girl you fancied in the schoolyard and giving her a load of old smiley gab. Then for her to turn around in front of all your butties and say: Did you clean the pooh off your smelly little brother today, yet? Just imagine how you'd feel.

The picture of a young lad shitting himself and a strange feeling of shame are all mixed up in the one now. Let me only get a whiff of Jeyes Fluid anywhere, and immediately I'm right back in that classroom and what happened to the two lads. I have never liked corduroys or sandals since.

School was a strange new place, and it took ages till I got my footing. Knowing Mikey, though, was great. We started school the same time; then sat together with the rest of the sniffling, snot-licking infants on forms at the top of the room round her big table, saying nothing, taking the place in. Stop that licking your nose with your tongue, she'd roar at one of us, and the other *uallāns*, from first and second class behind in the desks, would take to the sniggering.

Me and Mikey ate our lunches in the yard; then played Cowboys and Indians the same way we always did, except instead of each other's haggards and sheds, we were now stuck in one corner of the playground. We were herded in like sheep, along with the other infant scuts, by Ritchie Byrne and the big fellows who were keeping most of the yard for themselves, like they bloody owned it. See that line, says Ritchie. I'll give you a toe in the hole if you come over it. Feck off! There's no shagging line there. Then jump away – Ritchie's big boot is swinging in your direction. It was only a rule made up in the yard, not a school rule at all. That's the way things went.

Stick to the rules and everything's fine. No point having your arse kicked for crossing a line that isn't there, or getting into scrapes with big fellows twice your size and having your head boxed off. Stay in

73

where it's nice and safe. That's what I said after a few sore rumps.

There was the odd bully hanging about, just waiting to pick on small scuts; like a scald-crow hovering over lambs in spring, waiting its chance to gouge their eyes out. But he'd no sooner pick on us than some little mother hen from second class would run inside to tell. The Battleaxe would send for your boyo, and he'd get the shots – the one thing, at least, to be said in her favour.

Bit by bit, Mikey ventured out. He was a hit, right from the start, with most everyone, especially the girls. Little ones came over, all nosy about his black-as-soot curls, wanting to run their fingers through them; the way Ciss had done, that time back in our shed. The spunkier ones, with the scrawny legs, made ugly freckled faces at him and ran off, trying to draw him on to them. At lunchtime, the big girls would bring him into the shelter and jostle a place on the bench for him to sit down beside them, share their sweets and tidbits with him, then play with him: swinging and pulling his arms, flopping him up and down like they would a rag doll. A rag doll golliwog with long, baggy, flannel pants on was our Mikey, or a furry kitten maybe. The golliwog kitten would chase after a clatter of gangly turkey girls – all fluffed and puffed out on top and going gobbledy gobbledy gobbledy at him. Then some big turkey would run up from behind, catch him under the arms, swing him around and tickle the daylights out of him, sending him into fits. He had a royal time.

His pockets bulged with goodies cadged from the big ones. Fair play to him, though: he wouldn't think twice about giving you a Scots Clan or a gob-stopper. It didn't bother me then, either, putting out my hand for any of his leavings. I just took it as him sharing with his old buttie; didn't read any more into it.

Even the Battleaxe had a soft spot for Mikey: the one infant among us she'd look at when our turn came to be grilled. One and one is two, one and two is three, one and three is four . . . and on, and on, till we'd frighten the crows singing it. The only reason she was bothering her head now with us was because she was knackered, after hammering shite out of first and second classes, the old tyrant. Mikey was the one, though, who was asked the questions, and the one who got things explained to him. The rest of us were bystanders.

And, what better man for the job? He lapped it all up: the attention, the sweets and everything. Born into it he was. Little lord Mikey, meant to be the main man. Mam had said I was a little showman, going there the first morning, but I couldn't hold a candle to Mikey. The rest of us stayed slopping around in our little patch without him. Me and Willy Pecker Murphy knocked up a right bit of playing, chasing and all. We forced ourselves to be good old butties into the bargain, messing around both on our own and with the rest of the scuts.

I was getting used to the Battleaxe inside too. Even if she was callous with the bigger classes, shouting and slapping them and calling them dumb stupid stookauns for not answering out. She went down the back of the room one day with a knotty ashplant to slap Mag Brennan – a hardy snipe that one. Hand out, says she. As she raised the stick and pulled, Mag drew in her hand at the last second. The Battleaxe stuck the bur on top of the stick into her own leg. Good enough for her. She was a lot milder, though, on us infants. It probably had something to do with Mikey being among us. Saved by the presence of the precious one, what!

Eventually we made it on to the desks – the ones

with the inkwells – and started scratching and scraping with nib pens and ink. Tony *a bhuachaill*, says she to me, will you push over there *ins an suíochán*. And she'd hit you a dint of her elbow, sending you flying across the desk. The elephant on a tricycle in the circus – the picture in every colouring book in the world – that was exactly her, trying to squash that carcass of hers into a tiny desk. What'd happen, I wondered, if sometime she couldn't get back out? Probably stand up, she would, and walk away with the desk stuck round her waist like an apron.

Next thing, this big sweaty arm would land round your shoulders – phew, the pong off that! She'd grab your writing hand, pen and all, in her great paw, and squeeze the living daylights from your fingers against the pen-handle. Away with the two hands, off around the world together, scratching out joined writing and dipping for ink every other second. Keep the nib between the blue lines on your copy, she'd shout; up to the red line and down to the red line. A wallop then across the back of the head, sending whatever was inside whorling round, like slop down a plughole, over a blob on your page.

Again it was Mikey she'd spend all her time with. Would he get as much as a clout though, ever, for doing things arseways? Och, but you're a terrible boy you are, she'd say, grinning down at him, giving him little pats on his curls, letting on to be mad at him. Little mister terrible boy – the precious little git.

She'd start off talking to you in English, then break into the Irish and splutter away for ages. I didn't have a clue what she was on about, leastways not during those early days. Any time she spoke to me, it was about Aidan. Going on about how bright and all he was, how he could have made anything he'd wanted of himself; that I wasn't anything like half as *cliste*. And where is he now, *cá bhfuil sé*? she'd ask. He's going to the Tech in town, ma'am, says I. Then she'd go *tch tch*, and why wasn't he sent to the Brothers or even to boarding school? The same old yarn every day, not remembering she'd ever said it before. Times she'd forget herself altogether and actually call me Aidan. Disgusting, that was: who in their right mind, tell me, would want to be taken for Aidan?

At some stage, it dawned on me: the woman wasn't really all in it. The way she went on, like: leaping up off the seat in a tear, face real flushed, bursting out laughing – fast, high-pitched laughing – right there in the middle of a lesson, for no reason. She definitely wasn't right. Anyway, school, tough old station and all as it was, had to be better than being stuck at home, under the old lad's feet, and scared out of my wits of him.

6

CODD'S COTTAGE WAS THERE RIGHT NEXT THE SCHOOL. Only a stone wall separated the two yards. It's where Long Bob and Long Johnny lived. Everyone called them that, talking about them, but not to their faces. Each was only a long hank of skin and bone. Johnny showed the films in the hall, Wednesday and Sunday nights, and was hardly ever at home in the daytime. A flipping genius with machines, that man; could fix anything, and tell what's wrong with an engine by just listening to it.

Bob was a different kettle of fish. He was always staked out there in the cottage, like a rustler under siege in a cabin up the Rockies; the curtain moved when us cowboys took to the yard at lunchtime. Some awkward customer, that fellow. Couldn't stand the sight of young lads; and anyone under fourteen, going next door to school, was vermin to him, fit only to be hounded out of existence. Not that you could blame him, seeing as he got plagued so much. Lads were forever jumping in over his wall after hurling-balls, footballs and especially sponge balls. He made several attempts to put up a wire fence on top of the wall, but he'd no sooner have it up than some loodheramaun would climb it like a monkey, dragging the guts out of it; sometimes not even after a ball, only doing it for the lark to get Bob going.

All he seemed to do was grunt, roar and call hens. When he'd see you climb in over the wall, he'd run out the door shouting to terrify the daylights out of you. And you'd end up scrambling back over the wall, knees scraped and bleeding, but no ball. I don't think Bob ever wanted to catch anybody though. He always pulled up short, slowed down, when the fellow he was chasing was a fat slowcoach. His intention, it seemed, was to scare us off without the bother of having to deal with us if we were caught.

When Bob got his hands on a ball, well, that was that, the last you'd ever see of it. He must have had millions of them stashed away inside: all colours, makes and sizes. He could, if he'd wanted to, open a shop in the morning and make a living, selling nothing else, only balls. Every fellow I knew had lost at least half a dozen to him. But there was one thing we all liked about Long Bob: he never squealed on anyone to the master. No matter what fences were broken down or mischief was done – even if he caught the fellow red-handed – he still never told. You could torture that man till his limbs fell off and he wouldn't budge.

Whenever Bob was to be seen, and wasn't either chasing lads or pottering around his old ramshackle sheds, he was going choook chuckie chuckie chuckie, then choook chuck chuck chuck chuck, again and again. Must have had the best-fed frigging hens in the solar system. Not alone was he feeding them all the time, they also got their share from us: all the scraps of bread and half-eaten lunches that were thrown in. Some man for singing to hens, boy. He'd start off real high-pitched, then drop down a note with each call. That whining caper could erupt at any time of the day and go on for ages.

Ours was the nearest schoolroom to his yard: the voice would come trumpeting in, interrupting lessons, and off we'd go in the titters, driving the

Battleaxe mad. She'd put on her Jack Russell scowl again, turning over the whiskers and all. I didn't know it then, but Long Bob was doing it just to annoy her. They didn't get on, never spoke or nothing.

The real lark, though, was during singing practice. She'd have us flying up and down the scales: me, fah, soh, lah, tee . . . Then on the same note: choook chuckie chuckie chuckie chuckie would come blaring in. The sniggering would get so bad, she'd put lads to stand outside in the corridor. Cool off out there now for yourselves, she'd say. The corridor was a strange place. Every sound, even whispers, echoed, like how ghosts must whisper to each other round the grave-yard at night. Only thing was you'd hear Bob twice as well from there.

Then one day, standing in the corridor, I got this strange feeling about it all. Weird. Bob's chuckying was out of tune, out of time, with the Irish song *Beidh aonach amárach i gContae an Chláir* going on inside. Yet in another way they blended perfectly. Seemed like that, anyway, from out there: that place of hollow echoes hissing. Totally different things, and from different spots, were working together to make one big sound. Like you'd hear on Radio Eireann of a Sunday night: an orchestra or concerto, one of those things, except its many bits and bobs were always too much in harmony to be really in harmony, too made up.

That moment, though, was much more real. Had an order to it none of us, it seemed, was supposed to know about. Bob's going chuckie chuck was actually the main song, and the class song was only a background chorus. Older voices from the other two classrooms, as well as other sounds from outside – didn't know what they were – all had their place in the performance. The more each varied from the other, the better they fitted in and the more suited they became. All the various noises happening at the one time were really part of one mighty concert, the one sound. You'd want it to last.

> *Beidh aonach amárach, rattle rattle,*
> *Choook chuckie chuckie chuckie,*
> *I gContae an Chláir,*
> *Yes sir, no sir, don't know sir, six per cent sir,*
> *Choook chuck chuck chuck . . .*

Maybe every noise in the world was like that: different things making up one big concert. From school, houses, the whole village, town, the Tech

Aidan had gone to, and the sky – everything in its own right was maybe a single piece of one mighty orchestra. And was this in turn only a splinter of something bigger? But where did it all stop? It had to end someplace. This thinking had gone too far beyond me, but it was exciting.

I had this great urge to rush in and tell the teacher about it. Copped myself on, though, just in time. For feck's sake! Imagine telling all that to the Battleaxe? She'd put you into the middle of next week with a box.

One day a big lad from fifth class discovered a new use for Mikey, other than as a soft toy for turkey girls to play with. Because he was light as a feather, Mikey was easily lifted in over the wall by any big lad, and sent across Bob's yard for a ball. The big lad would reach down and hoist Mikey back over the wall; the whole operation over before you'd notice.

It was a treat watching Mikey dodge for cover: out from behind the barrel, across to a pile of sticks, in little short stabs of runs. He was so deft, Bob inside hardly ever noticed. Even the hens paid no heed, lifting their feathered necks only for a moment before going back to their business of pecking the ground; as much as to say, it's only our pal Mikey again, so no need for all that noisy clucking business. Same as how he was with the gangly turkey girls who wanted to play with him all the time. Sure was mighty with the birds, Mikey.

A threat to neither hens nor turkey girls; instead, he was the opposite – charm itself. Not a sweet honey sugar, iced topping, smother you all over charm – his was the real alley daley, breeze in the trees, fire in the grate natural charm. What people liked about him was he didn't push himself, or climb all over them with niceness. None of that. He'd worry you though: the close shaves inside in the yard, when Bob would suddenly step outside, almost catching him. What always saved Mikey was his calm head and his immaculate timing. He never panicked in there, least not that you'd notice; he kept low behind cover, moving only when Bob moved, holding out till Bob was gone. Mikey was a natural, and a real cool customer.

He was still the number-one ball gatherer when we went into fourth class – long gone from the Battle-axe's clutches. Mikey had remained puny compared to the rest of us, and was easily lifted in over Bob's wall.

Round that time, I had that trouble with the Slim Brien from sixth class, younger brother of tight-arse Minnie, the queer one Aidan had the hots for. It broke out more or less over Mikey. The Slim was anything but slim. His mother said he'd got fat from lying around the house doing nothing but gobbling all the bread that she'd lugged home from Murphy's shop. Bet you anything that's why Minnie's so scrawny, says I to Aidan: Slim nabbing all the food, leaving her to go half-starved. No wonder she has a bony arse. Did Aidan ever fancy hearing that lark!

A fair man for the grub was our Slim. When we were back in infants, he used go around nicking lunches on us. If there was meat, tinned salmon or anything tasty in a sandwich, he'd snatch and gobble it up, quick as he'd look at you. Finding only cheese or jam, he'd turn up his nose and shag the whole lunch across the wall to Bob's hens, leaving his victim to go hungry for the day. There was one thing in his favour, it must be said: the Slim was a fair old judge of sandwiches. Only the best would do Slim. I'd lost my lunch several times to that fat hoor, and always, it seemed, when Mam had packed something special: a bit of beef left over from a Sunday stew, with lashings of Yorkshire relish over it, or nice thick slices of ham with mustard on top. But your man had a fecking nose, as sharp as a bitch in heat, for sniffing out savouries like that. You could bring nothing tasty to school or he'd have it whipped away in a flash. I knew what the Slim was like.

I should have known better that day, so, than take what Mam was giving me. There's a nice bit of chicken between your bread today, says she. My mouth was watering all morning at the thought of the sandwiches. Half twelve and out we went, tearing down the steps to get a seat in the shelter. But sure as shit in a jinnet, your man pounced. He grabbed the lunch out of my hands, just as I was about to dive into the first sandwich, and made off with the whole lot. He went *yum yum* around the shelter, bragging: Will yous look at what I've got in my sandwiches today, lads?

The next day when Slim was kicking a ball, it went into Bob's yard. Slim called Mikey and hoisted him over the wall. Mikey got the ball, threw it back and waited for Slim to lift him over the wall again. But Slim had gone off, leaving Mikey stranded. Nobody ever did that – it was breaking an important rule – but Slim, the bollocks, did it. Mikey stood, mouth open, looking up at the wall, like a stud ass waiting on a mare, too stupefied to notice Bob heading out the door after him.

Not much time and no choice in the matter, I hopped in and gave Mikey a leg up the wall. Bob didn't want to catch us anyway: he was slowing down his approach to give us time to get away. We made it, cut knees, red faces and all. It was good to see the grin back on Mikey's face. I reckoned, though, it would probably spell the end of his great forays into Long Bob territory.

The day after that, coming out at lunchtime, our class was behind the ones from the master's room. I saw the Slim ahead, probably smelling the air, licking his lips and wondering whose lunch he'd feast on that day. I got this notion, a mad rush of blood to the head, and pushed my way towards him. Now was the chance to clock him. I caught up with him just before the steps down to the yard.

There he was on the point of taking the first step. Well, here goes, I says. It's now or never, and I stuck my foot in between his legs to trip him. Next thing, he was waving his arms grabbing at nothing, falling over. I threw myself after him, pushing him, to make sure he'd go down and not get back up to come after me. Went down like a sack of spuds, he did, his shoulder going sthumph on the concrete – his carcass had turned sideways during the fall, with me on top of him.

No way was he going to get up to come after me, I'd make sure of that. So I leaped up and sent my foot into his groin, as hard as ever I could. All the lunches, slices of chicken, the mustard and ham that were in that mound of flesh. My sandwiches – those were my sandwiches, they belonged to me. Why the hell did you take them? I shouted. I'd kick them to be damned out of you now, so I would. All I got, though, for my trouble, were these groans.

The next thing I was being pulled backwards by a couple of big fellows. Slim just lay there, a great slumped dumpling at the bottom of the steps, moaning. Get up, you big cunt, you're not that hurt, says I. But I knew he was hurt: it showed on the faces of the others, especially the girls, as they looked at me. He's to blame; what are yous gawking at me for? I began. But they stared, looked away and stared again. Then the regrets: oh feck, why did I have to go and do that? He didn't deserve it, did he? All that sort of thing.

The master made his way down the steps, pushing past a group standing with their mouths open. He told everybody to go off and play, do whatever they'd been doing before. He'd got the jitters; the froth was coming out the sides of his mouth and he had big mad flashing eyes. He always got like that anyway about things. He bent down over the Slim, and the Slim went aaah, and the master became more jittery. He called over a lad from sixth class and sent him off on a message. He looked in my direction. I met his look; I knew he knew it was my fault. So some lick had rushed in to tell.

The master's topcoat was brought out and laid over the Slim, as if the fat hoor needed more padding. Eventually the nurse came, knelt down and examined him. The master asked different fellows questions. Then he came to me.

I had a fight with him, sir, I told him. I pushed him and he fell down the steps. I never mentioned tripping him, kicking him on the ground, the sandwiches or what had happened with Mikey. Then the master blustered off with himself, leaving nothing sorted out. I knew there was more to come.

After lunch I slouched back into class. Our teacher, Mrs Mooney, who was the master's wife, started lessons as if nothing had happened. Five minutes later the master came in, all business. We'd stand up every time he'd put a foot in our door. There was only one thing on his mind, though – me. His eyes came searching till they landed on me, and he beckoned me out from the desk. Now I was for it. At least the suspense of the lunchtime wait was over. He had the stick with him. Let's get on with the beating, so. That's what I was in for, wasn't it? I felt the shivers, and hoped he wouldn't ask a whole rigmarole of questions: I didn't want anyone to see I was shitting myself inside. I thought about the two brothers that time in infants. Was that a whiff of Jeyes Fluid I got just then?

Are you aware, says he, you've put that boy in the county hospital? How do you feel about that? I was wondering how much he knew. His lips were all wet with spit and the white lather was still bubbling at the sides. You could see he was doing his best to keep in the rage and not draw out with the stick. Please, no questions, sir – I almost said it out loud.

I could picture Slim lying there in hospital, an ocean of doctors and nurses looking and poking their fingers in his blubber, saying: What species have we here – is this a whale? And he going oooh aaah, like in a comic. Bet he was sorry for all the loaves he'd eaten.

Master Mooney's voice boomed out: I don't know

yet what's going to happen in this matter. I'll deal with you after I see your parents. And I will be talking to the O'Brien family.

I'm sorry, sir, says I, even though I wasn't.

For now, says he, you'll sit in a desk on your own and do not come to school tomorrow till I see your parents. He spoke like the priest giving the sermon of a Sunday, and his spit was getting me full in the face. I was going to be drowned in it. He turned on his heels and marched out of the room; the class jumped to attention. That much, at least, was over. Mrs Mooney looked out over her specs at me, said nothing and just beckoned me back to my seat. A shrewd old tassie, that one. By right she should've been the boss in the place.

Before going-home time, the master came back in, handed me a sealed envelope and told me to make sure I gave it to my parents. The big curved writing said Mr and Mrs Cullen. I knew then I was in for it. Mam opened it, read the note inside and quizzed me up and down about what had happened. I told her the whole story. She said nothing when I asked her not to tell the old lad. A stupid thing to have asked, I knew; he'd have found out anyway and it would only make things worse if Mam was to say nothing.

He read the note when he got in, and I watched his face for signs. I saw the blood rise in the neck. That was enough: I was sure of what was going to happen. I burst out, telling him about all the lunches Slim had taken, and the way he'd left Mikey stranded getting the ball; that I couldn't handle Slim on my own in a fair fight – he was too big. I had to do something, I said, but hadn't meant to injure him or cause trouble. All the words came out in a rush: a last-ditch, desperate effort to ward off what I was in for. Useless though. And Daddy, I shouted between the flailing thumps, I'm sorry for all the bother I caused. But it made not an iota of difference. He muttered, between his teeth, about me being the greatest scourge of all time. The blood was up – the face of him! Looked like an orange balloon you'd see in the hall at an old folks' party.

Mam was shouting at him: Stop beating the boy! That's not going to make anything better! Too late, Mam, I says, he's already started. Can't help it, you know that; he's just not able to contain himself till the anger runs out. Bloody lugs! Why did they have to be so stuck out? Always the first to get the bang coming in from the side: the one that can't be seen. They'd ring the shagging head off you then, for hours on end.

It was time to escape again. Up the haggard and under the tree. The angelus bell was ringing. The sound floated up over the long grass and thistles and came through the gap in the evergreen. There it was calling out again: Come away with me. Drop everything now, let go, forget and come away to the other place . . .

I wanted to follow it off, away from there, to float up like a butterfly on a July day, carefree and light. I wanted more than anything for that to happen, but without pain. Ah, there was the difficulty: the without pain bit. I wanted no more pain. The two ringings kept going on all at once, becoming all the one sound. Then the bell stopped, and the lack of sound was back filling its place. That was all right too, I didn't mind; for nothing mattered a shite any more. And it became kind of nice that way: peaceful under the evergreen. I could've stayed there for ever, except the night chill was settling in around and starting to bite.

The letter had said my parents were to call and see Mr Mooney the next day in school, to sort things out. Afterwards, Mam filled me in about what'd gone on at the meeting. The Slim, it seemed, was lucky: he hadn't hit his head off the ground. He wasn't that badly cut up after all: nothing broken, just bruises, a fair amount of soreness and swelling. Shock was what affected him most, but he wasn't being kept in hospital, which was a relief.

What else was ahead of me? Was I to get slapped, or had the master got something else up his sleeve? No, says Mam. The master reckoned you'd got enough beating when he'd heard how well your father had taken care of that end of things. He wants you never to cause trouble like that again in his school, and to apologize to both Slim and his mother, especially his mother. That'd put an end to it.

The Slim stayed out of school for over a week, luxuriating himself. When he did appear back, there was no problem; he just kept away. The lads in Slim's class made no trouble either; they weren't out gunning for revenge or anything, and there was no sign of them getting together to come after me. I thought they might have, out of class loyalty. But no, it was the opposite to that. They were very nice about the whole thing, like I'd done them a favour, saying hello, Tony, and all smiles when I met any of them.

Strange, like, having big fellows out of sixth class noticing you, treating you as if you were one of them. They even wanted to know would I go out to the school field at lunchtime hurling with them, and if I'd like to bring a couple of the others along out of fourth class. So it turned out not such a bad move, after all, clocking the Slim like that. Your man too, Mikey said, had started bringing in his own sandwiches. He didn't bother me any more. Whenever I spotted him, he was hanging around the yard inside chasing small lads, a different one every day.

Me and Mikey and Willy Murphy brought our hurls into school. We were only put out-the-field, to send back overhit balls to the big fellows who played backs-and-forwards tussling around the goalmouth, but at least it was something, a step up the ladder. Then one day they called me in to play as a forward, in place of some lad who was out sick. It didn't take me long to get the hang of it. It was mighty scoring the odd goal and winning the ball. Good man, Cullen, there! Even Mooney, when he came out twice a week, training the lads for the schools' league, shouted: Young Cullen boy, that's the way to do it. The hurling was getting to be a right lark. And I liked Mooney for not keeping what'd happened against me.

7

GOOD ON YOU, PENDER BOY. YES, THE BOLD PETER HAS made it here. I just knew the man wouldn't let me down. He pushes through the crowd, with the bike going click click alongside him, right up to the back of the hearse. He then leans his bike against the churchyard wall and goes over to Mooney and the hearse driver, standing at the church gate, to talk to them.

The routine is to be what it always is for a funeral coming in: four able-bodied men, friends or neighbours of the dead person, to carry the coffin inside and wait for the priest to sprinkle it with holy water and read a prayer. Then up to the top of the church.

After a couple of minutes, they break up their

meeting. The driver goes to the other side of the hearse, opens the door and reaches in for something; then closes the door. Peter and the master go to the back of the hearse, stand and stare into the crowd and Peter goes in among them. What the hell is he up to? He's not going off with himself, is he? Not now when he's most needed round here. Hey, Peter, get your arse back here, boy. No, it's all right. He's only gone to talk to a few of the neighbours. He's coming back. Three men step forward out of the crowd and follow him up to the hearse. Mikey's father is one of them.

The driver opens the back door of the hearse and slides the coffin out real slow and careful. The man knows his job. The shiny coffin handles and metal braiding are cold to the touch, even through the leather gloves he has on: the man has soft hands. He leaves it for the other men to take the weight. And the wood veneer is cold as it passes into their hands – hard, weather-beaten hands like the flint in the pier caps nearby. These men, though, know what's to be done. Peter makes sure the coffin is balanced. He's the last man to take hold, and checks with each of them that they're comfortable. Now they're ready to move off as one.

The evening rose-light just catches the side of Peter's head as he turns round. The light, which sparkles off young faces along by the path, out here shows the ageing in Peter's face; it can't be fooled. It's the first time I've ever noticed any frailty in the man. The bottom rim of his left eye is slightly wet, while the flesh underneath is puffed. There's a purple tint to his chin and neck which I've not seen before either. He has to open his mouth to catch his breath, after the effort of moving off. That mighty specimen of a man, the well-designed machine – beyond destruction almost – that he once was, is now weak, unsteady and discoloured like a leaf in November. But he's still the number-one man around here; still in smooth control of himself.

The stories they tell of what Peter got up to in his young days are only mighty. Winning county medals, plucking balls out of the sky, travelling faster than what the eye'd see and turning around in an area the size of a sixpence to score against the very best of men – with only wellington boots on, because he couldn't afford leather studs, after spending all his money on porter. Yet the jar never stopped him from playing a match, never got the better of him. Hey, Peter, would it not be inclined to give you a sore head the next day and slow you down, someone'd ask. What? says he, real indignant like. Do you not know no better nor that? There's nothing as good as a mighty feed of porter the night before a match – whets the appetite for the game.

From one sport to another: from hurling to women. They say Peter was a devil for the women. Can you imagine – must have been some sight, boy – Peter, dancing and waltzing around the floor with loads of posh women and all. Still in his wellingtons, what? He could do better any time in them old yokes than most other fellows wearing great fancy leathers. Besides, if he did happen to step on a woman's toes, with them things on she'd never feel it, now would she?

When it comes to getting things done in this place, Peter is the one person people expect to step forward and take charge. On an occasion like this especially, he can be trusted to know the proper routines and to make sure they're carried out.

Steady as she goes. Four strong men, two on either side, step gently towards the church gate. You could balance a glass of water on top of the coffin. And Mrs Brennan is back on the job, pulling the bell-rope.

Sound vibrates everything as people gather in closer round the back of the hearse. The men are at the church gate, shuffling slowly along the tarmac, wheeling round to get through the gateway; then in along towards the chapel. Now stark against the light, this unit of men and coffin is like a strange insect that has just climbed up from the bowels of the earth.

Following on, the two aunts are with little Jimmy and Aidan is between Ciss and Mam. It looks like Mam is away out of it; that it is only her shell there walking. The old lad is over there too. The people behind shuffle along after them. The procession moves in past the school classes at either side, and on till they get inside the door. Then the whole shebang comes to a dead stop.

It takes a while for your eyes to adjust to the scarcity of light, and you're inclined to look at the flickering candles and the sanctuary lamp. The men carrying the coffin have their heads bowed, while they wait in front of the priest and two altar-boys. In his white surplice, Father Breen stands real solemn-looking, a prayer book open in his left hand with his right hand over the back of his left. All's gone quiet; just the odd cough. The only thing moving now is the draught in from the open doorway, and what it stirs. It's far colder here than outside in the evening air.

Mikey is the altar-boy carrying the holy water and sprinkler. So, that's where the little sleeveen has got to. I should have known. Tucked in beside the priest there for safety. What? Look at the black curly head of him, will you? It matches the black frock he's wearing. A right little maneen of a priest altogether. And the soft-smiling face as pink as the flesh of a tiny newborn rat. You'd think butter wouldn't melt in its mouth.

Some difference, though, his face makes to the priest's dried-up old puss and wizened skin. And the scaldy bare top on his reverence: bald as a baboon's arse, except for a few grey strands a mile long growing at the sides. Wait till I get my hands on that Mikey, I'll wipe the angelic smile off his gob and soften his cough for him. Stand back there and let me at him.

At the bottom of the church, Father Breen does that thing now with the sprinkler and holy water, with the help of your man beside him. You better watch out now, Father. That little hoor will be after your job before you know it; sneak it out from under your nose when you're not looking, he will. Don't say you weren't warned, Father.

The priest mutters some prayers from the black, leather-bound prayer book. The red, white, yellow, green, purple and blue silk page-marker strings hang from the top of the book, and then blow up across the back of his hand. The breeze also catches his white surplice and tosses it back against the more rigid cassock underneath. He prays on regardless.

I said, Father, that that fellow would be after your job. Especially if he gets wind of the big fry-up you have for breakfast most mornings with two women waiting on you hand and foot. Oh, that'll do now, Father. You go on reading them prayers; you're doing a powerful job there, keep it up.

It doesn't take Father Breen long to get the prayers said. Just as well: you can't expect them men to hold on for ever. Himself and the altar-boys take off, slow-worming it up the aisle ahead of the coffin. Everyone's glad to be moving in from that biting breeze round the doorway. The coffin itself is not too heavy, so it's been no great strain on the four holding it there the while.

The stained-glass window behind the altar comes closer. A great jigsaw puzzle of a thing. I love the way it lights up of a sunny Sunday morning, the way the purples and browns come alive. It would cheer you up when that happens, especially if it's in the middle of a heavy sermon – a Father Breen special. No light coming through now. Not a spark of life there.

8

THE MILL WHERE PETER WORKS IS DOWN UNDER THE road, at the bottom of the valley. It's tall and magical, like something straight out of *Hans Andersen's Best Fairy Tales* – a book I once cadged off Aidan, and which Ciss then took from me. It has stone walls and a round red-galvanized roof like a hayshed, only much bigger. The small windows have diamond-shaped panes, and shutters – also painted red – splaying out like the wings on Mam's brooch. Pierce the owner has this *grá* for the colour red. Aidan reckons it was a job lot of old shite paint that Pierce picked up on the cheap from a hawker passing on the road.

There are these massive timber lintels over the two

double doors – yet more red. They'd remind you of a giant's monstrous arms, but so bowed, weighed down with carrying that ocean of stonework, you can almost hear them creak. You'd wonder for how long more those timber arms could hold out before the whole lot came crashing down. I couldn't bear to look up, any time I passed under them.

To one side, there's this great brick chimney tapering as it goes straight up in the sky – a weird and gigantic cannon to bang down monsters flying past during the shooting season. Except it never does; it's only there on-the-ready, always pointing upwards. I hoped no great dinosaur bird would ever fly by. One blast out of that thing and the whole place would shake to bits, and come clattering down in a pile of stones.

The waterwheel, though, is the life and soul of the place. Tarred black, pinned up and out from the gable nearest the road, it's a whopper of a wheel and rattles the whole building when it moves grudgingly down, around and up again. Endlessly rumbling, like thunder not far off. The water gushes out, from under the road above, into the long black timber chute that carries it across to the top of the wheel. And there's a trapdoor in the floor of the chute to let the water spill out before reaching the wheel. Lately, that door has been left open most of the time: the water pours off and flows away in the tail-race and you don't hear the thunder, just the dead sound of water splashing. The life is slowly draining from the place.

I started going to the mill with Aidan a few years ago. Once a fortnight or so, barley was brought there for grinding into meal to feed the stock. Cows and fattening cattle are the right greedy guts for meal; they can't get enough of it during the cold weather. Aidan was only mad to be showing off his driving: any excuse to get out on to the open road. He'd yoke up the small trailer to the tractor and reverse it under the loft steps in the yard at home, no bother, whistling the Beatles.

He'd call me and up we'd go into the loft, bucketing grain into small sacks. Make a lug on the mouth of each sack, tie it with binder-twine, haul it on the hand-truck out to the top of the steps and lower it into the trailer. Then off with us like hell, up the yard and on to the road, Aidan revving blasts of blue-black smoke from the exhaust of the old grey Ferguson. Still going strong as ever, Aidan used to say; with the best of a diesel in her and not burning as much as a drop of oil either. Loved that old tractor, he did.

How long have we got that one for now, Aidan? says I. Queer ignorant, though, the fellow: he wouldn't even let on that he heard.

The sensation of sitting on the bags of barley, bouncing like mad from all the potholes in the road, was only mighty. The one thing about those bags: there was no bother filling or moving them, they were so small. Not like the brutes of barrel-sacks they used on the combine; there was some lugging and dragging with those things. Aidan would perch himself ahead on the tractor, like the king of Leinster, driving it for all his worth, head slanted against the wind blowing in our ears, listening out for the engine racing against the control of its governor.

He could as easily have been the captain of a pirate galley, riding the threshing waves round Cape Horn. Or some great astronaut, no bother, steering that mighty craft off into the depths of space, dodging between lines of enemy fire, on a mission to carry those sacks of gold dust, special delivery, to the moon. No limitations to what we could have been, no restrictions. Shout out at the top of your voice, boy, loud as you were able: the sounds wouldn't register above the splutters of the tractor exhaust. Least that's the way it seemed. It was real freedom, just like the night long before when I'd gone back into the kitchen, into the light, to find Aidan dancing away with Minnie the twig. The very same freedom that had filled the kitchen then was back: a freedom bubble round the tractor and trailer heading to the mill. A mad, wild bubble that carried us floating on. We'd definitely have to bring Ciss with us sometime: she'd been part of it, too, that time before. It would make things more exact, more of an anniversary celebration of complete freedom.

No matter what'd happen, where I might go in the world, I'd never let myself forget that mighty feeling. It called for a name there and then, and I christened it the Minnie the twig dance feeling, in memory of the time I'd first tasted its freshness. I'd tell nobody this name either, nobody at all – only Ciss maybe; because she, too, had probably felt the same way. And you could trust Ciss.

I went cuish cuish cuish at the enemy approaching on either side, protecting the captain alone in front from diabolical attacks on our ship. The ugly enemy kept coming and I killed them off, one by one, till I reached the leader, their captain. His was a face

I knew: it was none other than the ugly puss of that ancient fiend, Captain Old Lad. And I got the greatest pleasure giving him one helluva long, torturous death in painful agony, a death lasting all the way to the mill. And he pleaded for mercy in all sorts of different ways, begging and crying: Please, please spare me. But all his pleadings were refused.

I'd lower my sword slowly down over the back of his neck, touching flesh with sharp steel, till at last he'd crawl on his hands and knees before me to beg for a quick clean end, to be put out of his misery. His wish, though, would never be granted, the end never finally coming his way. I'd keep him there forever kneeling, feeling small and ashamed of all the beatings he'd ever dished out. I don't think I even once finished him off. The taste of revenge, though only imaginary, was so savoury I wanted to make it last.

Never quite finishing off a job was something new; it had this odd sort of appeal to it. Delaying an ending, dragging it out, had an enjoyment all of its own, especially when you had the power to give it that final swipe any time you wanted. But when you finished off a job that was the end of the satisfaction and you'd have to move on to something new. All the better then never to finish a thing. It was like driving a nail almost all the way into a piece of wood but not quite clinching it, leaving it for one last blow; only never coming back to give it that blow. That's the sort of power I'd've liked to have had over the old lad.

But was there not, maybe, another side to this? The notion of ongoing, unfinished business might've been great, especially if it worked properly; yet was there not the danger of taking it too far? You could go overboard with that, you know, and end up having too many irons in the fire. When nothing would ever get rightly done, with everything left in the balance, like, and you wouldn't know where you were with anything. It could all get so out of hand you might never finish a blessed thing, not even a game of hurling. Imagine not finishing the game, even when winning, just to hold on to the satisfaction of being ahead, and missing out on the pleasure of the win itself. Frigging daft! You mightn't even go back home, say, if you were sent to the street on a message. Some lark, though, that'd be: boy disappears with pan loaf on road home from shop. Sure would keep old Vronnie Byrne in business for ages; she'd have to invest in a new mouth.

Not sure I liked some of those notions I had while

sitting in the trailer. Must be losing my marbles, I says. If anyone else was to go on like that, they should be taken. For a while at least, there on the road to the mill, the bubble of freedom would stay intact as Aidan, out in front, drove the Ferguson on with the throttle opened out to the last.

Yeah, there's the mill just coming into view. The chimney was still cocked up to the sky, and not a blooming shot fired out of her, boy, since she was built. Ne'er a great monster bird had flown over, so that old cannon might've had a chance for one good blast before collapsing in a heap on the ground. Least that way she could've gone out in a blaze of glory; like your man General Custer making his last stand against the Indians.

Aidan pushed the silver throttle forward, and the engine spluttered back to a tick-over. The speed, the noise and the whole shebang ship just ground down. The bubble had burst and the show was over. We turned in off the road and down along the sharp-sloping drive to the mill. The weight of the trailer lurched forward on the narrow slope, trying to force the tractor to pick up speed. But the gearbox was having none of it: the back-wheel tyre grips crunched stubbornly against the stones on the track. All thirty-five horses inside her held firm, and the king of Leinster took her down and around, nice and easy.

Aidan drove out from the building, straightened up, backed the trailer into the mill opening and stopped the engine. The clutch pedal clacked against the stopper bar as he lifted his foot, swung his leg over the steering wheel and hopped down.

We were right under a pair of trapdoors way above in the second floor. Peter Pender shouted down, and this chain came dropping through a hole in the middle of the trapdoors. Me and Aidan lugged the bags up on their ends and tied the chain round the middle of the first one. Right, take her away, Peter, Aidan shouted. The chain tightened and the bag rose up till it reached the doors, dragging them open with it. The doors flapped shut again with a deadened thud, and the bag was gone from view.

When Peter finished taking in the bags, he came down on to a floor slightly above our level, almost facing us. The talking started up. We agreed the day the meal would be ready for collection first, then he slagged off Aidan about girls. Soon the topic changed and Peter went all serious. His forehead wrinkled like drills in a field, eyebrows full of flour dust moved up and down and the eyes seemed to deepen further in his head. He was, of course, on about hurling and how it should be played, like nothing else in the world mattered a jot. The reason he was alive was for the hurling, to see it practised right – better than the state of the game these days, anyway. As if he were the guardian of its skills, he took on the manner of a harsh old missioner you'd see here in the street, every third year in October. Take the old greats of long ago, boy, could they hurl, says he.

Came to life, they did, as he talked. When he was my age, mighty men swung narrow-bossed sticks of a late evening. They made long shadows across Springmount fields. Men who'd worked horses and stooped over ploughs all day danced out on to the grass again, refreshed. Great hands would reach into the night air to snatch a ball from the sky, swing and strike, the way fork lightning strikes – you could almost hear the thunder. Limbs moved smoothly, arms as strong as forged steel and hands like the flint from the fields they worked.

Old ghosts were still playing gigantic matches, condemned to step out and hurl, time and time again, till the day arrived when nobody would talk about them any more, no one would remember or give a curse. Only then would their long overdue rest come, and they might stop haunting fields this side of the Blackstairs. Even ghosts must get fed up doing the same thing every evening. They must wonder: when will new heroes ever come along to take our place and give us a break, for feck's sake?

It was the same yarn every time we went to the mill. Peter would launch into a tirade on the state of hurling, then drift off, remembering the deeds of great men from somewhere out of the past. Not that his yarns weren't exciting to listen to; or maybe they weren't that exciting if you'd heard them a thousand times over. Something else, though, about the man would hold your attention. A sort of burning in those steel-blue eyes of his that was ready to tear the heart out of anyone who might dare stop him in the middle of his remembering. He was as fierce as any bald monk you'd ever hear from the pulpit during the October missions. The way Peter told it was what mattered: you had to listen, even if you didn't want to. What he said went.

Some old lads slobber on about the old days, stuffing it down your neck, how hard the times were when they were young, the way they had to work, *not like the youth of today*, and all that baloney. You couldn't listen to them tired old hoors: drive you scatty, they would. But Peter was different. Though the years were piling up, slowing him down, he was as mad as ever for living. And it was natural for him to be in charge of everything around him, of both the living and the non-living.

He'd remind you of a big house: the ivy, the high windows, the half-moon glazed light over the hall door and the cut stone steps. The house still mighty, despite the plaster coming away, the cracked ridges and split Blue Bangor slates that slip sideways, letting in the weather. Still grand, in spite of age, but where the age is against it all the same, for it has seen its glory days. It's been a long time since those slender windows let in sunlight on any children there at play. The wine curtains might still be elegant, like the plaid skirt that hangs off Brudgie Whelan's hips; enticing, even inviting, a hand to touch. That's not something you could quite bring yourself to do, to meddle with the undisturbed quiet. But the drapes, you can tell, only cover up the rot that gnaws on the timber casings and frames; and some day the whole lot will come away from the stonework supports in a pile of dust. For that powder is already building up on the curtain linings, and floats out everywhere. A million billion dust warriors, suddenly caught in shafts of sunlight, fly their dazzling speck-ships in a never-ending war to rot the world and break it down till nothing's left but dust.

Such a house deserved only a man like Peter for its owner. He had the know-how to be in charge, to keep things right. And the remainder of each of their great lives might be spent in the satisfaction of the other's grandeur.

The first time I heard that my old lad was called Sniggers was from Peter. Sniggers Cullen had the makings of a right hurler too, says he, one time he was on about how the game should be played. Sniggers, that's some queer name, I says to myself, and I had to stop and think: it had cropped up before sometime, but where? Yeah, that was it, during one of them bloody awful tearations they were having. When Mam became real vexed, she'd roared: Go away from me, Sniggers, you old bastard. I never thought it might be his nickname; just some handle she'd concocted there and then to sting him with. That was Mam for you: she could put all makes of words together when the humour took her. I'd never heard anyone else call him that – they called him Jimmy, mind you, to his face.

In all our trips to the mill, Peter never gave much else away about the old lad. I'd wanted to know what Peter thought of him, ever since that first time I'd heard him call him Sniggers. What he did eventually say was: I can remember when the thing happened with that Doran fellow. The way he said *that Doran fellow*, spitting it out of him, it could as easily have been *that lump of dung there*. The same contempt. I wondered what the poor bastard had done to fall so low in anyone's estimation.

Sniggers and Doran, it seemed, were great buddies when they were young. They went everywhere together and got up to all sorts of things. As young men, they travelled the country on bikes to *céilíes* and house dances. Until something happened: a row over a woman, it was. The next evening they were in the hurling field, training for a match the following Sunday. Sniggers hit Doran with the hurl. Your man lost an eye and that was that. Sniggers never again took a hurl in his hand. Don't know which was worse, says Peter, your man losing the eye or hurling losing a talent like Sniggers. He never gave anything else away. At least we had something to go on: the bones of what had happened. All that was needed was the information to fill it out.

One other person, though, was bound to know the ins and outs of the story, and was probably prepared to tell it too. I had to figure a way of getting it out of her, without making it obvious I was fishing for information, or else she'd clam up. She was inclined to talk only about the things she wanted to talk about. That was the problem.

9

OLD VRONNIE BYRNE WENT UP TO THE STREET ALMOST
every day, yet you'd scarcely notice the few items in
the bottom of her bag. Shopping was just an excuse to
be out. Fresh news was what interested her, not fresh
food. The black shopping bag hanging off the hip,
bandaged tight round the wrist, turned her fingers
pale as the ivory in knife handles. Friday and Saturday, though, she'd have more to carry than normal,
allowing for the shop being shut on Sunday – except
after Mass when it was too crowded anyway, with all
the children looking for crisps and sweets.

Since her house was only down the road from ours,
it was easy enough to keep an eye out for her comings
and goings. The old iron gate rattled off the stone

striking block and squeaked at the hinges when anyone went in or out her yard.

The chance came one Saturday morning. I heard
her gate opening and ran up the yard to check. Yeah,
there she was wobbling on down the road, in fits and
starts, and stopping to turn and look around, take
everything in or see if there was anyone coming.
From a distance she was like a grasshopper: the
spindly elbows pushed up by her sides. I had to step
back behind the pier of our gate in case she spotted
me. There was plenty of time to catch up with her, at
the rate she travelled. So I went into the house, took a
screwdriver from a drawer and shoved it down my
trousers. I gave Mam the excuse of going to look for
the screwdriver I'd left after me the evening before in
Tommy's bog – one of the fields we used to hurl in. I
then tore off after Vronnie.

And where are you going this hour of the day, eh?
she asked. She was standing looking at me before I
caught up with her, hands to the knees propping
herself up and forefingers pointing straight down.
When I walked up to her, she had to swivel her head
round to look up at me. A screwdriver, eh, says
she, when I told her. She repeated the answer after
you and then stuck an *eh* on the end, turning what

you said over on its back, making sure of the truth in it. Sometimes she put the *eh* on the end of a question – checking out your answer before you even told her.

And how did you lose that now, eh? What were you doing with that now when you were hurling, eh? Fixing the band on your hurley, eh? And do you think you'll find it, eh? Would somebody else not be inclined to have it picked up before you, eh?

Grate on your blasted nerves, she would, especially when the lower lip goes smack, up and down outside the upper one, licking the taste off it, savouring it. Shhhlurp. The cheeks suck in and out as she purses the lips, non-stop opening and closing like fish in a bowl. With all the questions she was asking, it was going to be a job steering her off the business of the screwdriver, let alone getting her to talk about the old lad.

On down the hill with us, like we were cronies all our lives. Then up the far side, till we reached the gap to Tommy's bog. I thought she'd never stop the blooming questions. Listen, Vronnie, says I, if I happen to find the screwdriver fairly quickly, I'll follow you up to the street if you like, give you a hand carrying the messages. I needed to spend more time fishing out of her.

She stopped and looked up at me with those round rheumy eyes: Aw, thanks very much, son. Aren't you very good now, like your father before you when he was your age.

Yes! Here was my chance at last. If I could only manage to keep her thinking about him, before she'd wander off on to something else. The best thing, I allowed, was to get away from her that very instant, to give her more of a chance to think about him and what he used to be like. When I'd catch up with her again, she'd have so much stuff about him in her head she'd be only dying to talk.

There I was going around like a right one inside in the field, staring at the grass, letting on to be searching, while Vronnie stopped at every low gap in the road hedge, hands to the knees to straighten herself up, trying to look in. Checking, I bet, in case I was only codding her about the screwdriver – you'd have to be up early now to cod that old one. A right piece of play-acting, and along with the hope of getting the information I'd wanted from her, it felt like ether going to my head. I checked that Vronnie wasn't looking, pulled out the screwdriver and threw it on a few yards ahead. Then I let out a roar. There it is! I have it. Made sure she was watching when I picked it up. This time I carried it in my hand.

She called me Jimmy when I caught up with her. Well, Jimmy, says she, I see you found it, eh. Did she think it was Sniggers back there in the field or what? Imagine calling me Jimmy! Old people, though, can go like that sometimes; they lose their bearings as to what generation they're in and get mixed up about who they're talking to. The same way as the Battleaxe used to take me for Aidan back in infants, except in her case she wasn't all there even at the best of times. So I didn't mind too much Vronnie being like that.

There was no bother getting Vronnie to talk about him now. As decent a chap as you'd find, says she, until he met up with that Patsy Doran. The girls were all mad about him but he only had eyes for the one; not that I know what he ever saw in her. It wasn't Mam she was referring to, was it? Oh now, I could tell you a thing or two, says she; I know what happened there all right. No, it definitely wasn't Mam.

Mrs Rourke below of the hill – old powder puff herself – was a Jane Quigley, one of the Quigleys of the mountain, before she married Jimmy Rourke. Ashamed of who she was and where she'd come from, she used to do the law-de-daw when she went anywhere, to the dances and that, trying not to let on she was off the side of the mountain above. No fear of old Vronnie being ashamed of herself, not on your life. You couldn't help but like that about her: what you saw was what you got. Jane Quigley was the opposite: a phoney, she must have been.

Sniggers and herself hit it off at a dance one time, and started seeing each other. That fond of her he was too, says Vronnie, he never bothered with another girl while courting her.

When Vronnie said *courting*, I got this queer picture in my head of the old lad, his big hairy arms around gangly Mrs Rourke, squeezing the lard out of her. Hardly able to speak, she was, with all the air being knocked out of her lungs. Just about managing a dainty little squeak: Please, Sniggie dear, you're breaking my bones, you know I'm not rough and tough like some mountainy woman. I'm frail and tender like a film star. So please, dear, be gentle just like me, dear.

I pictured him laying his big gob on her lips, covering up a mountain of lipstick round about her mouth. But no matter how he tried, he couldn't manage to cover them completely: they'd pop out to one side or the other, going phopp, those blood-red lipsticky lips. Scary things floating, phopping around, from a nightmare or a Dracula film. Long-winged bats – only red, not black – same shape and all. Everything in the picture got smudged with red, and suddenly I felt glad that my mother was full-bodied, ruby-lipped and big-hipped. A warm woman. No, not just glad – over the moon, I was right then, that Mam was my mother, and not that long rubber-faced statue, Jane Quigley. If Mam was here this minute I'd tell her what she meant to me. Then again, maybe I wouldn't. You couldn't bring yourself to say things like that to your mother.

But Jimmy Cullen wasn't the only fellow she had the eye for, says Vronnie. Liked the men sure enough, did our Jane, and one of them was Jimmy's own friend, Patsy Doran. The same Patsy, a nice fellow he was to know, all right. Oho, the way she said that! Vronnie could cut when she wanted, saying the opposite to what she meant, and with the voice raised just the right amount. Give you the creeps, she would. But somebody else knew the carry-on, says she; brought the story to your father, told him to be in this particular place on a certain night of the week and he'd find out for himself. I couldn't help but wonder who that somebody was.

Vronnie was wound up. He found his Miss Jane all right, says she; herself and that Patsy fellow in the hayshed together, stuck like glue. She was staring at her hand: the second finger crossed over the fore-finger. Then she looked at me to see if I'd picked up on her meaning. But you're too young to know what I'm on about exactly, aren't you? says she, turning her head away like she was only wasting her time talking to me. I didn't know then what she meant. I know now though.

Vronnie went on. Nearly dropped, he did, when he saw them together, the poor man. How he didn't do them in there and then, I'll never know. I suppose he was too shocked. The next time they met though, in the hurling field, he went for Doran bald-headed and nearly killed him – not that that would have been any great loss either. He had to be pulled off him.

What happened to Jane Quigley? says I, hoping she'd keep on going. Oh, now that'll do, says she; as fine a babbie she had as you ever did see. Vronnie looked at me, checking again. She snuffled her nose along the sleeve of her coat. But not before marrying

Jimmy Rourke below of the hill, she said. She made sure of that all right. The poor man who wouldn't harm a fly, and old enough to be her father into the bargain. Didn't know what he was letting himself in for, the crater, when he got landed with that one, let me tell you. Two for the price of one: a great catch sure enough. Anyway, you shouldn't be hearing this. You're too young.

I got the feeling she was sorry for saying so much, or maybe she'd copped on that I'd been fishing out of her. But then her voice softened: You'd hear it sooner or later anyway, wouldn't you, so what's the differ?

Oh, Mrs Rourke below of the hill, is it? I said to keep her going. Sure, she's a nice woman really. I tried to sound surprised it was the same person she'd been talking about, letting on it was only that instant the penny had dropped for me.

Nice woman is it? says she. Bless your innocence, child, is that all you know of the people round here? A nice woman, he says. Vronnie was back on full throttle. Her face flushed up and swelled, and she straightened her back more than I'd ever seen her do before. She was livid. I hoped she wouldn't draw out at me with that old shopping bag.

As we walked to the street, there was no stopping Vronnie's tongue. She gave out stink about Mrs Rourke. But there was nothing else new to what she had to say, and by the time we got home again I was glad to get away from her.

10

THIS YEAR IN SIXTH CLASS WOULD HAVE BEEN MY LAST IN National School. I was looking forward to getting out of the place, to escape from Mooney; I'd spend the rest of my life hurling, and chasing women like Aidan was doing. Only in the last two years I started getting interested in the girls. Fascinating creatures they were, like swallows in summer flitting around everywhere, full of life.

It was nice and easy talking to the girls in our class. No need for horsing around, jostling or acting the git. And you'd talk about serious things you couldn't with the fellows: wishes and dreams. They understood those things. Any good-looking girl too, especially Brudgie Whelan there, always had this extra appeal.

You'd want to be near her and be noticed by her, because you, sure as hell, noticed her. Maybe you'd even dare think of running your fingers through her long hair, or touching the white flesh of her neck where her hair throws a shadow behind her ear. The most natural thing ever: wanting to put your arm over Brudgie's shoulder when she was upset, when Master Mooney had been cross with her – though that wasn't often. Dismal to see those clear, sunshiny-day eyes fill up and stare into the ground.

Even when there was nothing the matter with Brudgie, you'd still want to put your arm around her; a sudden urge would come over you, seeing her there looking so pretty, sedate and all. But you couldn't walk over real serious like and do that to a girl, no matter how much you wanted to. Only a pure *leatrom* would chance that. The fellows would think you were gone soft in the head.

There was, of course, a way round it. The thing to do was act the gom, play the halfwit and jig around the place, but not overdo it, lest she turn sour. Then you'd move close to her, sneak an arm about her spindly waist and give her a light squeeze. Flash the *Black and White Minstrel Show* grin, and sing: *I asked her for a little kiss, down by the riverside, down by the*

132

riverside, down by the riverside. Get her going like: wheel her around in a half-turn. The way they go spinning and singing in the old sloppy films; the ones that'd drive you to tears, watching them on television of a Sunday evening over in Mikey's house. The same films, though, were just right for giving us a lark at times like this.

This carry-on would have to happen with the other lads in the class looking on. There'd be the usual big whoosh off and a slap across the head from Brudgie, with the lads going: Oh ho hoo, Tony boy. Oh that'll do you now. Oh we know what you're like all right, oh ho hoo. Then you'd give them the bad eye and do another dance for their benefit, as much as to say: Now, me boys, there's one more notch for yous to remember me by when yous are knackered-out old men in soot corners, boring the shite out of lads with stories from the past, while I'll still be on the go. A great feeling entirely. You'd wish Peter Pender were there to see the lark. Where's my wellies?

The whole thing used to go down a treat. But you hoped Brudgie would see through the lark to what your intentions really were; that she might respond, though not in any obvious way: she'd just say something with those eyes, twitch up the corners of her mouth to let you know she saw no harm in it, and didn't feel she was being made a show of or anything. You hoped she'd actually like all the jig-acting; would give you something to dream about going to sleep. Then again, by the time you'd shuffle into bed that night, you'd have forgotten what happened maybe.

But this business of what the big fellows, Aidan and them, got up to with girls, when they were out with them, was a whole mystery to me. Sure, we heard all the dirty stories, hints and laughs from them, but I was still none the wiser. I didn't even know if Mikey knew. He let on he knew but I don't think he did, and I wasn't going to ask him. Yeah, we told each other yarns about girls' diddies and arses, and nudged each other, behind his mother's back, when anything came on television over in his house.

Maybe a man and a woman, on the screen, would lie down in long grass, hardly anything on. His hand would stroke her hair, her face and move down along the rest of her. He gets more in earnest, like, and slaps the gob on her. The stroking gets firmer and faster, up and down. Mikey gives me a dig but his old one has spotted him, so he keeps a straight face. Your man rolls over on top of the woman, pinning her to the ground – in case she might run away. But that's all you'd ever see. The minute any real action starts, the camera would rise up on to branches and leaves. You're left gawping at an ocean of bloody trees blowing their heads off and not another glimpse of the pair on the ground. Nothing, only the sound of moans and groans and rustling leaves, and Mikey's mother going tut tut tut.

It was the same at the pictures in the hall. A man and woman would stand beside a silk bed the size of a hurling pitch. Again, when the two would start the business, the camera would move down on to their feet, as if the whole film were really all about feet. One of her legs rises up out of view, then the other. Her shoe falls off. You wait – could have your dinner eaten in the meantime. The second shoe drops. Where the hell did she go? Up along some rope ladder you didn't happen to see? Maybe she's an acrobat? She is surely. Then his legs, one by one, would disappear. A shoe falls off on to the white rug – always a snow-white rug. Time for another dinner break before his other shoe would land. For feck's sake! And you were still left in the dark about things.

As it happened, Minnie Brien, Aidan's girlfriend, was a right one for explaining mysteries, the best teacher of all. I tell you, boy, that one knew her stuff.

In the shop, one Sunday after Mass, there was a crowd of us pushing to the counter to get served. Minnie was standing to the side talking to another girl. I bought a choc ice and moved around to that side of the shop. Minnie was too busy gabbing to her friend to notice anyone, least of all Aidan's brother, overhearing her.

She was on about the fellow she'd been out with the night before, how he'd been such a great laugh and all. But his hands had wanderlust in them, says she. Some hands – oh, he was awful.

And did he produce Fagan? her friend asked her.

Did he, feck! says Minnie, quick as a flash. Couldn't keep him in for love or money. The two of them shrieked out laughing so hard, they had to cross their legs and go up and down, like long-necked geese pecking grain, to keep from exploding altogether. They grabbed each other's arms and fell around the place in hysterics.

The mad tear to the counter had suddenly stopped. All faces turned and gawked at the two who had just dropped through the ceiling from Mars. The other one put her hand to her mouth and muttered to

Minnie: A bit cold last night for that sort of thing, wasn't it? More hysterics.

Minnie guffawed out of her: A big purple Fagan, as far as I could make out. Purple from the cold.

They were about to launch off into the fits again when Minnie spotted me. It was like she'd been shot through the heart, the look on her face. Or when Long Johnny's film projector goes on the blink. The sudden end to action on the screen; nothing left, only this still ghost gaping out at nothing in particular, and then gone. Her mouth hung open, both hands leaped to her face, and the fingers went propping and puckering up the flesh of her by now white cheeks. Her eyes went in a daze.

Only when I was outside the shop did I realize it wasn't Aidan at all she'd been talking about. He'd spent the night before, himself and the old lad, sitting up waiting for a cow to calve, a heifer about to have her first-born. They couldn't leave for fear she might run into trouble on the birth. It was some other galoot Minnie had been out with then. But I wasn't going to go home and tell Aidan what I'd heard. I didn't give a curse if she'd been out with a million fellows while she was supposed to be Aidan's girl. He didn't own her or anything, that she couldn't do what she liked

137

without his consent. And it was all none of my business.

But then she made it my business, didn't she? I was scarcely a few yards over the street when she came running and calling after me. She knew I was Aidan's brother, but I didn't think she knew my name. It's pleasantly strange to hear your name being called by a person you don't expect to know it, and whom you've never actually spoken to, especially when that person comes after you as if you were their best friend. She was panting and saying: What you heard us talking about back there . . . well, it wasn't true. We were only making it all up, for the crack, like. Only for a bit of a laugh.

She was half looking at me and half looking around her. None of the old guff out of her she'd had in the shop. You won't tell Aidan, will you, sure you won't? She was nearly down on her knees pleading. That must have been the way Father Breen meant it when he said off the pulpit on Sunday: Get down on your knees and beg for mercy, and not just once but keep asking. Minnie kept begging, looking for an answer.

I could've waved my little finger, boy, and she'd have jumped. A great feeling of power entirely. I wasn't putting her much at ease either; not that I didn't want to. I didn't know what to say or how to deal with it. She wouldn't give up, though, till she got an answer one way or another. So I blurted out: I'll say nothing if you promise me something.

Yes, anything, says she. Just you name it.

Will you tell me what goes on between men and women when they're out courting? Oh shite, what had I said! The question had shot straight out from the back of my head somewhere, and not so much as the screed of a thought behind it. Too late. It was already blurted out.

Talk about being annoyed with yourself! I could've pulled my blasted ears off for saying such a stupid thing. Left myself wide open, caught out, the way Minnie must've felt when she spotted me in the shop. I'd handed the controls back to Minnie, and she knew it too; the way she raised her head and darted her eyes through me. She was right back in charge now. I was out in open country, waiting to be shot down. Wished I could hide under a stone, or duck under a pile of soft hay.

What do you mean? says she sharply, interrogating me with the eyes.

You know what I mean, says I, slobbering like a

pet lamb sucking. What's the big mystery about? What goes on, and all, alone in the dark? What you were saying back there in the shop.

Now that was it; that was all the talking – slobbering – I was going to do. I'd explained my side of the deal and she could either take it or leave it; the choice was hers. I'd already made enough of a *leatrom* of myself with her. I wasn't going to make it worse, no matter how much eye-quizzing she did. It was her was in the shite anyway, not me, and if she wanted me to keep my mouth shut, she'd have to trade.

For a second there was a sign of the frightened look back in her face, but only for a second. She stared at me, threw her head back and laughed. Yeah, she was laughing again, though nothing near as loud as before. Then she stopped, stared at me again and smiled. I tell you, boy, she was queer good on the glares and stares. You could feel the eyes going through you like a bloody X-ray machine searching out fractures. If you promise not to tell Aidan – she was thinking hard while saying it – only if you promise, mind, and you must keep the promise. She was trying to make the most of what she seemed to have on offer. It reminded me of the old lad bargaining with the cattle-jobbers after the winter.

The way he'd haggle his best to get that last bullock, the scrawny one that hadn't fattened up right, into the same deal they'd struck over the good cattle.

Listen, I got to go, says she. The queer one is standing waiting on me.

Fair enough, says I. Goodbye, so. I turned for home the way the big whiskey-faced jobber, in fawn pants and brown scuffed shoes, might do in our yard every spring when himself and the old lad laid into that same game of bluff.

No, wait, don't go. You didn't promise, says she, grabbing me by the shoulders and digging her claws in. She was getting flustered and her eyes were pleading again.

You didn't tell me, says I, what I've asked you.

I'll tell you what, says she, letting her hands collapse by her sides. You call over to the priest's house next Friday round four o'clock and I'll talk to you then. Mrs Brennan and the priest will be gone to town shopping and you needn't worry, they're always away on Friday. Don't forget your end of the bargain.

All right so, says I. A bargain then.

Minnie smiled before she turned to go. She had a nice smile.

She walked away real funny like. Her back cheeks were full out, round, tight against the flowery material of her minidress and rolled from side to side with each long step. High heels clip-clopped off the tarmac. It was the same as watching the back end of one of Murphy's thoroughbreds, the way she high-stepped away to the shop. The same slender legs too, nearly; the only difference was horses' knee joints were turned back to front. Or was it hers that were back to front? You'd get mixed up thinking about it and looking at her. No way was that the same scrawny-arsed Minnie I'd been slagging Aidan about; that Minnie with the skirt hanging off her bones, like it was tied to a clothes line. I didn't know what to make of her then, as I gawped after her.

As if gawping at her was exactly what she'd expected, didn't she toss round her head to catch me, and say: Don't forget now, Friday evening at four, see youuu. All right so, says I. She lifted her hand, gave a dainty little flutter of painted nails, smiled at me from behind the hairline and off she waddled. Was this frigging Marilyn Monroe, our own living doll, Marilyn Minnie Monroe? Wow.

Now thar she goes
Just a wokking down the street
Singing du waa diddie
diddie dum diddie du . . .

She was nearly back to the other one when
I noticed her gait change. Couldn't say for sure
how: the long stride was gone from her walk maybe; not so much hip swagger, or was there more
hunch to her shoulders? She moved, then, the way
Mam does when she's worried and unsure of her
step.

Could it be, because she was working with Mrs
Brennan in the priest's house, she had to go around all
stiff like: part of her job? Maybe she was meant to
walk in a particular way: a uniform style of walking
for religious people and those working near them.
Judging from the way Father Breen preached of a
Sunday, it wouldn't do for her to be swagging them
mighty fine hips too much around his kitchen. No,
he'd have none of that. Plenty of rashers, sausages
and fried eggs, but no hip-swaggering in miniskirts,
please. I hoped to feck she wasn't going to start
wearing black, or go sprouting a cocked arse on her –

fine the way it was, thank you. She wouldn't look well in black.

Right then, the belly was rumbling and falling out of me. I'd have to get home soon or I'd be late for the dinner and maybe get nothing to eat.

11

SIT DOWN THERE, SAYS MAM. SHE PLOPPED MY PLATE OF dinner on the table, right in beside the old lad. The others were nearly finished. Mam herself was the only one not yet catered for; always the last to sit down, and long after she's handed everybody else up theirs. And seeing the leftover bits she gives herself, you'd want to scream at her: Put a proper dinner on a plate, same as you do for everyone else, and treat yourself for a change. You'd be raging with her but only ever bring yourself to say: Ah Mam, is that all you're having? Even mention that, she'd throw back the head and stare you down with the brown eyes as much as to say: Stay back, mind your own business and don't dare touch. You weren't going to be let

traipse around her private estate. That was the other thing about Mam.

She had a world all to herself where she spent a fair part of her life. I wasn't sure what it was like there; quiet probably, like the sanctuary in a nuns' chapel with the glimmer lamp: a safe, untouchable place. She was the keeper of the keys. Every so often, she stepped back into our lives to put dinners in front of us, and do things. Then off she'd go into her refuge again, leaving behind only the shell of a body for us to talk to and be with. This was happening more often. I'd never seen her so withdrawn in herself, but you'd not dare ask what was wrong. Her wish to be left alone was always met, even by Sniggers there – as far as I knew.

Standing by the cooker, picking scraps on to a plate for herself, she looked taller than she was. Head slightly bent, a lone thin figure, more like a stranger than our mother. I wanted to shout at her: You're not the only blasted alien round here, Mam. The more of a stranger she became, the more alike we became. That's how it felt. Did she see that though, did she see that there might be anyone else in the same boat? But then I thought: No. Gone beyond feeling, she was; had about as much feeling to her now as a turnip. How could she, after turning into a blasted robot? Another pale piece of shagging rubber, like powder-puff Rourke. Oh shit, I hoped she wouldn't start all that lipstick crack. Wouldn't the old lad love that; some phopping then he'd have inside in the room at night.

I was there a few minutes, gulping down buttered spuds and gravy, slurping and slobbering like I'd never got a bite, when whack! across the side of the head. The shock eased, but the waterworks were up and running. I felt trickles down the outside of my nose, and the drops floated on the gravy. Then I got light-headed or something, and thought about nothing only gravy and bubbles; the way they refused to mix, even when stirred around with a fork. I tried spiking and bursting them, but it was no use. I wiped my nose off the back of my hand, as slyly as I could manage, and sniffled away.

He muttered into my ear, in a low voice through his teeth, something about me needing to improve my table manners. I didn't take in all he said, but I felt the menace in his voice. He'd whispered because he didn't want Mam to catch on to him: she'd only kick up a shindy. Ciss got up from the table and disappeared like a shot; Aidan and little Jimmy had already gone out. Only me and him left there then, ignoring each other worse than strangers, and hating one another. I kept my head bent eating, or Mam would see my face. The one thing I didn't want was trouble for her, and he wanted no trouble from her. The dinner was gone tasteless.

His grating voice was the last straw, nearly. I thought I'd puke on the spot. I wanted to scream: Leave me alone. I've had enough of you, you bastard! I held out, but only just; went on eating slowly while trying to let the silence do the screaming for me. The hatred sent its roots into my bones. It felt cold.

Then this thing in the head started up. A kind of fog, a squally mist full of grey dots settled in, and a buzzing noise; a faint coming on. Except it wasn't a faint: something else that had a numbness about it. I felt the shivers, freezing almost, even though my forehead was sweaty and I could hardly budge. It came from out of the blue, the way a March sky suddenly fills with clouds and darkens over. The dots of grey flickered on the inside of my eyes like the bubbles on the gravy, only many more of them. Then it lifted, just like that, gone as quickly as it had come.

*   *   *

After dinner, Mikey called and Ciss came back in. Eyes all lit up, she was going round like a sheep with the gid. For once I was glad to see Mikey at the door, tapping a ball on his hurl. Any excuse to get away from King fecking Baluba sitting beside me, himself and his bushy shagging apeman eyebrows. Ciss plagued the feck out of me: what were we doing and where were we going? I snapped at her: Go ask Mikey, seeing as you have the hots for him. If it's Mikey you want to know about, ask him out straight yourself. She hadn't the nerve, so was asking me instead. I was sorry, right away, for saying it. I didn't mean to embarrass her in front of Mikey anyway; she deserved better. It wasn't her fault she didn't see through him. She'd been taken in by him, from the days of the Cowboys and Indians.

I grabbed my hurl, gave him the beck and the two of us hightailed it up the yard and down the road before anyone knew we were gone. It was great to get away and suck in the breeze crossing down off the Blackstairs, hitting us full in the face. Warm blood flowed through my veins again. I think Mikey felt like that too. He gave a quick spurt, ran on ahead and reversed down the road, hitting the ball back to me. We tapped it back and forth, on our way down the hill, till we reached Rourke's gate below.

Suddenly something came over Mikey and changed the easygoing pace we had, as if he'd just remembered an urgent message. All excited, he ran up to me, hand to the side of the mouth in case he might be overheard, though there was nobody else around. He muttered on about old Rourkie inside, and what she might be up to this time of a Sunday. I didn't know what he meant; I had no interest in her business, certainly not after Vronnie telling me the yarn. Since her son had emigrated – her husband had died many years before – she lived alone in the farmhouse, right where the road starts to dip steeply down the hill. She didn't mix much with the neighbours, and not at all with any of our family – good reason not to, I suppose. But she and Mrs Doyle were great cronies; Mikey's mother was always stuck in there. Mikey, too, was in and out doing messages and bits of jobs for her. I reckoned he must have known the house inside out, and I was right.

Come on till I show you, says he. Leave your hurl there by the wall in case we need to make a quick getaway. Always thinking ahead of himself, that lad. It sounded exciting, a dare or something. But all he'd say was: Shhh, come on. His finger up to the lips. We went quietly, half picking our steps across the stone yard, trying not to look suspicious lest someone should stick their head out the door and catch us. Laurel and frigging Hardy, how are you, not in the halfpenny place with us, says I, and I couldn't keep in the sniggering. Damn it, says he, will you go easy or we'll be caught. Through the porch and into the darkness of the kitchen. It took a while to get used to the half-light.

It was the most modern kitchen I'd ever seen, straight out of the pictures. You'd think you were in America, boy. Two rows of orange-coloured presses, one above the other and a space between them, all lined up square against the wall. A long steel sink and taps shining away there, laid in over the bottom row of presses. Snug under the chimney breast was this great cream-coloured Aga, flue going up the middle, control knobs and gauges like an aeroplane. Beside the presses and at the same height were two white-enamel, box-shaped gadgets. But I couldn't tell exactly what they were.

No half-measures there, boy, nothing spared. Queer different from the kitchen at home – the big rotting dresser, the bockety washstand in one corner and the old whitewashed walls gone black from smoke. No big dirty open fireplace in Rourke's, or fanners you'd spend the day turning to get a fire going. No specks of soot falling on top of you of a rainy night.

The only good thing about the chimney at home was that you could throw back your head and look up at the sky. With Luxembourg on, the lights out and the stars peeping in, the world took on a different shape. Like the day in the school corridor years before: all the various sounds making up one concert. Every sound in its place with a reason for being there; each thing as vital as the next, and any one person as important as the next. You knew you were seeing the world the way it should be, or the way it might be, if you had any say. The light-headed feeling, the stars and all, would disappear as soon as a puff of smoke floated up from the fire, and that'd be that.

The kitchen I found myself standing in was some place, though; would put you dreaming, wishing for things.

There was a nudge from Mikey, letting me know we weren't there to admire the kitchen. He winced up his face and pointed to a door right in the middle of the timber-sheeted partition. The door was so like the partition, you'd hardly notice it but for its shiny brass doorknob. So there was another room behind the partition, and someone inside too: muffled voices. Time to be going; I was a stranger here.

I was about to hightail it when I felt Mikey's tug on my sleeve. So off we went doing the Laurel and Hardy shuffle again: me behind Mikey tiptoeing through an archway at the far end of the partition, and into another room. Oh, very fancy in here as well; a dining room, like in a mansion. A big table against the other wall of the partition room, a white table-cloth draped down over its sides and a sheet of glass lying flat on top. Brown high-back chairs around the three sides of the table waited for gentry to plant their arses on them and tuck into a big feast.

Imagine sitting there, I says, a napkin from the neck of your shirt and elbows in tight by your sides, all proper like, while running an eye over the utensils to check they're clean and set right. Call the waiter. Is the venison nice today? And the coffee, is it strong? I'll have my afters now if you don't mind.

Another nudge of the elbow from Mikey. He moved one of the chairs out, placed it gently to one side, got down on his knees and crept in under the table like a toddler. Some toddler! What the hell was he doing? He stuck his head out from under the tablecloth and beckoned me to follow. Plenty of room there for the two of us to hide: you could've fitted an army in there, boy.

A queer caper this was turning into. Two infants crawling around under Mrs Rourke's dining-room table of a Sunday afternoon, instead of being above in the village at the match. For feck sake, let me out of here before I get a dumb-teat rammed in my gob, says I whispering. But Mikey wasn't minding; he was too busy pointing again. Next thing, he prised a board from the partition facing us, not making a sound; a piece that'd been sawn out before, and just left back. Probably the electrician pushing leads through. How had Mikey sniffed out this spot?

It was hard to see anything, down so low, and it was dark inside in the partition room. But there was something there all right. What looked like trousers, yeah, and shoes on the floor over there in the light. Then it dawned on me, we were looking right in under a bed, a big hooring ship of a bed. The sheets and bedspread dangled in ruffs and puckers over the sides: an old sailing ship out on the ocean, sails flapping in the wind. Captain Bligh's ship, that was it. Looking up, you could pick out the rigging: lines of

shiny wire-mesh springs running the length of the
bed in a wavy pattern. The whole thing was mushing
and creaking like mad, up and down, in and out. The
old ship was in full sail, going like the clappers. First
Mate Fletcher Christian, please sir. Up on deck right
away, sir, and see what's the rumpus. All sorts of
moans and grunts and aaghing were going on up
there. Must have been running each other through
good-o with swords and daggers – fierce slaughter.
Some mutiny on the *Bounty* we had on our hands
there. Any minute the fat-faced old captain should
get lobbed overboard, like in the pictures.

The mutiny was in full swing as Mikey whispered:
Come on. So out we crept – Mrs Rourke's two fine
infants – one after the other, the tablecloth brushing
over our heads, and back to the door with the brass
knob. Whoever was in there had forgotten to close
the door fully behind them. Let's have a peek, says
Mikey. Don't be daft, says I. But he was already down
on his hunkers and gently pushing in the door. I stood
over him, peering through the slight opening he'd
made. Two right peeping Toms we were.

Old Captain Bligh was well and truly gone from
his ship all right. He was out there in the middle of
the ocean, swimming for all he was worth. You could

see the shape of his rump going up and down in the
water, while his back and shoulders arched, stiffened
and pushed up. Doing the breaststroke, he was. Will
somebody send out a lifeboat for that poor hoor
before he drowns? I wanted to shout for the lark. But
it wasn't the sea, or Captain Bligh – that lad had been
dead for hundreds of years. It was Mrs Rourke's
rump and shoulders see-sawing up and down there
under the pink candlewick bedspread. I knew because it was her big head that appeared at the top of
the bedspread. And whose but the bold Pasty Doran's
head that lay back there on the pillow under her. A
big grin on his puss, like it was the opening of the
shooting season after months of waiting.

We could see only the back of her head from where
we were. Her red hair was matted and tangled, not a
bit like what you'd expect it to be. Couldn't be certain
it was her, till she moved her head sideways. Some job
to keep in the laughing. When I looked down at
Mikey, he was fit to burst as well. So out we had to
get before we gave ourselves away. We were on the
road again, with the hurls in our hands, when we let
go with the sniggering.

I did the oddest thing then, without knowing why.
There were these roses, wild scraggy ones, hanging

down over Rourke's wall outside on the road. Using the front of the hurl, I chopped one off, ran back in and shoved it, stem first, into the keyhole under the brass knob. It wasn't so much a dare, more a mark of some kind; the way a dog, leg cocked, squirts a gatepost to leave a mark.

I was back out in a flash. Mikey gawped at me, like I'd turned into a head of cabbage. Nothing was said, we just took to the fits of laughing, right the way to the village, and tapped the ball to each other: back and forth, back and forth.

12

THE PARISH TEAM WAS PLAYING A MATCH. THEY'D HAVE to win out the junior championship before turning senior. But they were never good enough to do that, least not in recent times. The nearest was ten years before, when they'd won out the district and made it to the county semi-final. They were badly beaten in that match and never really tried again. This year they'd roped in Peter Pender to train them, although no one believed that even he could improve them. The match, a practice game against a team from over the hill, was only in preparation for the first round of the championship. It was well under way by the time me and Mikey got to the field.

Peter stood on the sideline, halfway up the pitch.

Head bent, fists bulging in his trouser pockets, he turned his back to the game and made a kick at the grass. His team was getting hammered. What would you expect? Our fellows were like barrels on legs, short stumpy legs. Their jerseys were too tight to go down over their haunches, big baulks of haunches like store cattle in winter.

Master Mooney used to say: When the Firbolgs – the pot-bellied tribe – lost the Battle of Taiteann against the invading Tuatha de Danaan long ago, the survivors must have all come here to this part of the country to live. He was only jeering at us in class. Maybe there was some grain of truth to it, though, the size of our lads. Some warriors! Their problem was movement: they couldn't run for skins.

The opposition, in their blue-and-white jerseys and starched-white knicks, were lean and lanky. All legs and elbows, bits of joints sticking out everywhere and not a pick on them. Like buck hares, the big gamey shaggers chased every ball. For each long, bandy-legged stride they took, our fellows had to take two steps to cover the same ground. They'd solo upfield, weave in and out between our lads and strike the ball sweetly away in the air.

We walked behind a string of people watching the match, and up to where Peter was standing. This was the place to be, to get the inside information on how the lads were doing and if they'd be ready for the championship. When Peter wasn't shouting at the team, he stood talking to Red Bill. Then Long Bob Codd appeared. You have your work cut out with them lads eh, what? says he in the big deep voice; his way of saying hello. Don't I know it, says Peter, by way of saluting him back. How's she cutting there, Bob? says Bill, straight to the point. No hedging around or fancy hellos from him. Bob just looked at him and nodded.

Peter went in over the sideline on to the pitch and shouted: Moove the baaall will youuu. Hit it on the ground, Tubsy! Then Red Bill screeched out: Hit it along the ground, you shagging waster youuu, as if he was a one-man-backing gospel chorus bellowing out *amen* after the lead singer. Again, in case your man outside didn't get the message, Bill sang: Tubsy son, you couldn't pick it up if it was a blooming sausage on a plate. And *amen* to that too, Bill, says I. This black curly-headed fellow, in blue and white, came flying up and swiped the ball from under Tubsy's nose. Once more Peter turned his back to the game; head down and eyes shut, he made another kick at the grass.

When the game ended, Pecker Murphy from school came over, going mad to get fellows to hurl with him. I gave him a slap across the arse with the hurl. Feck off with yourself, Pecker, I says.

He didn't though, he just stared at me with the cow's eyes. What's wrong with you? he said.

There's nothing shagging wrong with me, Pecker Willie boy, you little fat-arsed Firbolg. That's how things felt.

Our lads were getting dressed, over at the ditch, behind a row of cars with doors and boots open. Feet on chrome bumpers, rumps on bonnets, they bent over tying their shoelaces. Eyes down, lower lips out but no talking, Sunday ties were reknotted without checking in the mirror, and no sprucing up of appearances. No one cared. Nobody would remember those Firbolgs.

Me and Pecker and Mikey didn't talk either. We kept on hitting the ball to each other. It was kind of soothing: blocking, tapping and striking the scuffed leather lump, like the beat to some ballad as old as the hills. Then block, tap and strike again; you'd forget everything else. The zip of the leather through the grass was the only sound that mattered, as the blood flowed comfortably, warmly through the body. Same as looking at the stars up the chimney: everything else was forgotten in the rhythm.

Then Minnie Brien and her friends came by. I'd spotted them earlier on, over by the sideline, shouting at the lads hurling. They'd picked on the black curly-haired fellow from the other team, the way the turkey girls used to pick on Mikey in the schoolyard long ago. Every time he hit the ball or did anything, they giggled and screeched behind the tight flat palms of their hands. It hadn't mattered to them that he was on the other team or that our lads were losing the match. Interested only in what Fagan there did, because they'd liked the look of him. When the teams had changed sides at half-time, they followed him across to the other sideline.

Here they were again, wobbling along over the soft earth. They lifted their legs like cocks treading hens – no place this for high heels – a pile of long flamingo-pink legs in miniskirts; some with round hips while others were scrawny. One set of hips was heading straight towards me.

Hello, hon, says she. How's the hurling?

How are you, Minnie? Long time no see, says I. Not since this morning.

You didn't tell him, now did you? she asked.

No I didn't, says I.

Aw thanks, hon, and don't forget Friday, says she. And away with her without stopping, curving off back to the others.

You're terrible, you are, one of them said to her.

Another said: She likes 'em queer young now, don't she?

Yeah, she'll be into the pram after them next.

Yeah, wheeling the pram, more like, if last night is anything to go by. The one she was with in the shop that morning said that.

Can't even hold her water so she can't, says Minnie, making a swipe at her with the handbag. Minnie tried to chase after her. But her heels got stuck in the sod and she tumbled forward. Hands and feet on the ground, her backside was cocked up in the air, matching the rump shape of the mountain behind. It was like she was doing press-ups, except she wasn't doing them right and was wearing the wrong gear.

One of the fellows togging in – Tubsy that Bill had roared at earlier – whistled, then shouted: Go on,

Minnie, show us a bit more; are you in training for tonight or what?

That shagger, of all people, had no right saying that. I shouted at him, without thinking: You, you big pot-belly waster, didn't show much yourself, did you, when you had the chance?

He made a shape at coming over after me. The minute he did, Minnie and the girls started laughing and jeering at him about the big tough man he'd become since the end of the match. That shut him up, and he went back among the lads and the cars.

Minnie looked over at me, did that little finger-wave thing again, and I reddened. The girls walked off with themselves, while I stood gawping after them. Mikey was watching me slantwise like a hawk. The beady-eyed cunt missed nothing.

Me and him took it nice and easy, heading down the road home, round suppertime. Coming near Rourke's, I said: Will we go in and have a gawk, see what's happening inside? I wasn't going to; only said it for the laugh. Passing by the gate, we saw her sweeping outside the door, swishing the twig like mad, threatening every last grain of dust in the universe not to dare come near the place.

We were gone twenty yards past when she stuck her head out the gate and called Mikey back. He'll be with you in a minute, she shouted up to me. That was all right too, her not wanting me to know their business. I didn't mind: she was great friends with the Doyles while she hardly knew me from Adam. I was curious nonetheless. When the two of them went into the yard, I sneaked back to the gate and stood behind the pier peeping with one eye. She'd left him standing outside the door. Being such friends yet leaving him standing outside, I thought, was strange. Or was it? Oh ho, maybe there was someone inside she didn't want anyone knowing about. I had this picture of a head on the pillow.

I could imagine him there at the dining-room table, a fork in one hand, a knife in the other and both pointing straight up. A napkin tucked in under the collar of his shirt, the gent waited for his plate of crispy rashers, plump bronzed sausages, black pudding, two fried eggs and at least ten slivers of crispy fried potatoes. *Oi think Oi'll have tea with moy fry this evening, madam, if you don't moind. Oi'm quite hungry now. Oi've had rather a busy day out on the ocean wave.* He'd wink the one eye – should have a patch over the other – and go on codding her. And I was picturing Patsy Doran wearing a blue-and-white jersey.

Mrs Rourke came out with a bar of chocolate in her hand. What did she do only break it in half, shove one piece down the breast pocket of Mikey's coat and hold on to the other piece herself, closing her hand round it as if someone was going to grab it. Bloody hell, woman! Did nobody ever tell you about chocolate? It melts like shite in your hands.

I didn't let on a thing till we were well up the road. I was testing him out to see would he say anything, or share it. Then I gave him a slap of the hurl across the breast pocket, and felt it hitting off something solid. Hey, what have we here, old son, says I; I might be wrong now but that's very like the sound of chocolate. I kept tapping the pocket. His face went a shade of flamingo pink. It was the first time I'd ever caught him out, and I was going to make the most of it.

Oh Mikey's got chocolate, Mikey's got chocolate. Eh Mikey, is it Turkish Delight or Rum and Raisin? Well, boys o'boys – I was trying to rub it in worse – if it isn't a bar of plain and what: not even a full bar? Oh! Mikey, that's terrible, she wouldn't even give a fellow a full bar. Terrible! That got him going.

Temper temper, I teased, and ran ahead up the road, letting on to be scared of him.

The house was like a morgue. Mam was gone to my aunt's, as usual of a Sunday, and had brought Ciss and little Jimmy with her. Aidan was out doing the yard-work, before his supper and heading off for the night – to see Minnie maybe. Heaven knows where the old lad was.

I was glad Mam had somewhere to go, though, besides being forever cooped up inside. Getting out always did her good; it brought the colour back in her cheeks and made her more talkative. I looked forward to her chirping on about how they all were over in the aunt's house. I used to love heading off there on my own with her, back in the old days. She'd take me by the hand, start singing on the road and get me to join in with her. Always the same song, never any other. It was as if she didn't know any other.

Let him go, let him tarry, let him sink or let him swim.
He doesn't care for me, and I don't care for him.
He can go and get another that I hope he will enjoy,
For I'm going to marry a far nicer boy.

Mogue Doyle

He wrote to me a letter saying, he was very bad.
I sent him back an answer saying, I was awful glad.
He wrote to me another saying, he was well and strong.
But I care no more about him than the ground he
walks upon.

There was something in the way she used to attack it, getting me to stride along with her and stamp on the words. We'd pound away, our hands held swinging with each step over the dust on the road, of a fine Sunday, as if we were a secret army for defying things, the song's words our only weapons: me and her, and the summer bumble bees that hoored off the dandelions and thistle tops in the gripe alongside us. She was the sort she'd have you singing there with her in no time. She had a way about her: could get you to do a thing and you wouldn't realize you were doing it hardly. That was all a long time back.

Right then, the only sign of life was the old silver alarm clock, roosting up on the shelf of the dresser, on three splayed legs. Tock tock tock . . . Tocking out the last of the day. The sound of it got me going: *Let him go, let him tarry* . . . I thought about Mam in her fawn coat, sitting on the arm of the couch, ready waiting for him to go to the pictures – when they used to go to the pictures.

The goings-on inside in the room at night, too, had long since stopped. There was not so much as a cheep out of them now – except for the snoring. They talked loud snores at each other across the darkness for most of the night. The odd outbreak of silence in between felt sudden and unexpected.

Any minute she'd show her face in the doorway. It was Aidan, though, who came tearing in, asking was Mam back yet. Was he fecking blind or what? He cut a slice of bread the size of a doorstep, buttered it, spooned jam all over it and went out through the porch, eating. I turned on the wireless. It crackled, probably feeling the worse for wear like everything else round here. I tried to get Luxembourg. No luck. I gave it a hoor of a thump, but still no luck.

Then, *Come on and hear, come on and hear, Alexander's ragtime band. Come on and hear, come on and hear, it's the best band in the land* came crackling out all of a sudden.

I was afraid to change it in case it shut up shop altogether; so I left it alone. I tried to sing out, *Let him go, let him tarry, let him sink or let him swim* to the air of this thing. And I thumped away with my leg off the arm of the couch.

Mam appeared in the porch with the two lads. Are you gone mad or what, says she.

I switched off the wireless, took myself up the stairs and plonked my carcass on the bed. I don't give a shite any more, I said; I mean about all the shagging changes around this place.

13

WILL YOU LOOK AT THE MASTER THIS MORNING, WILL you? Sitting up there full of himself, in the seat behind the lads, the white hair all sleeked back on his head. Who the hell does he think he is, Elvis Presley or what? The skin is puckered up beside his eyes: crow's feet – Elvis with crow's feet, oh Momma, what a man; I'm all shook up. He has fifth and sixth classes arranged: the yappers in front of him where he can keep an eye on them, and the quiet ones in by the wall. The school has taken over the front seats of the church on the left-hand side, the women's side. Any moment now Father Breen will come parading out of the sacristy, behind the servers; then the show will begin. For begin it must, this funeral Mass.

The last of the great last-minute, the usual last-minute, one-minute-behind-the-timers have just blustered in, after sorting out most of the world's problems. They fluster themselves into their fixed, rightful seats – same seats as every Sunday. The place is full of invisible signs that say: This is my seat, keep your sweet fat A off it.

We're under starter's orders now, so ready for the off. Oh no, we're not; there's a few more coming in. Some more stragglers: the later-than-laters, tiptoe-ing along. They'll be late for their own funerals, this lot. And making more noise, squeaking up the aisle in their crêpe soles, than they would wearing hobnail boots. Everyone turns to gawk; to see who it is, as if they don't know, or haven't already checked whose squeaky crêpe soles these are a hundred times before. They haven't grown horns since Sunday, have they?

Now you'd hardly hear a pin drop, it's gone so quiet. I suppose the coughing will begin next. They're the greatest people of all time for coughing, and old Vronnie is the leader. A spate of dry coughing will come tuttering out of her, like a machine-gun prodding out rounds of ammo, echoing back off the ceiling boards in the rafters. It only ever starts in earnest when the priest goes up in the pulpit. Vronnie will go tut tut tut . . . You'd think she was going to preach, the way she clears her throat. Father Breen opens his mouth – then tut tut tut, the guns are off firing at the ceiling. He's got so used to it he now opens his mouth on purpose, making a false start, to let them cough away; then waits for the place to quieten, not a word out of him till everyone's gob is well and truly zipped. Off he'll tear then like a bat out of hell; no false start the second time. Same yarn every Sunday, and it'll be no different today.

Ah ha! There's Brudgie in by the wall. Hey, lads, mind your knees there. That's it, keep in, I want to get past. Hey, Willie boy, how's the pecker hanging? Doing any hurling lately? Ah for feck's sake, Willie, put a smile on it will you, or you'll have us all in the doldrums. I'm off over to see this girl here on the end. Might as well be talking to the wall: he can't hear me.

Hello, hon. How's it going, hon? Now don't start, or say: You're terrible, you are. I'm not going to pull you out to the aisle, or make a show of you by acting the maggot; we're not in the schoolyard now. Look, all I want is to sit here and whisper. Is that all right? Looking queer well though you are, you know that? Ahh, the times we used to have. Mighty, weren't they? Hey, Brudgie, your knees are cold – look how blue they are. Let me warm them up for you. Listen, Brudgie, what are you going to do after sixth class? The convent inside in town, then what? You once told me you wanted to be an air hostess. Is that still on the cards? You know, I'd love to be a soldier, so I could go fight the communists in Vietnam. I'd shoot every last bloody one of them, from there to the North Pole, cuish cuish cuish with my machine-gun. That'd be some going, wouldn't it? Listen, if I got wounded or anything, would you feel sorry for me and come nurse me, would you? Ahhh! . . . Would be great though, wouldn't it: you an air hostess and me a soldier.

We might even run into each other sometimes, like. When I'd fly to America to join up, or maybe on my way to the war zone. I'd be sitting there in the middle of the plane, my tommy-gun in my hand, and who'd come waltzing down the aisle, only yourself. And I'd say: Well hello there, if it isn't Miss Brudgie Whelan all the way from Ireland? You wouldn't recognize a bit of me in the green combat uniform and the big helmet with twigs sticking out the side; with only these two whites of eyes peeping out, and grinning like mad at seeing you. The others would say: Who's that dame you know from back in the old country? That's sure one helluva fine-looking doll. I'd jump up out of my seat, and you and me would go fandango-ing up and down the plane. We'd show them, wouldn't we, hey, Brudgie?

Did I ever tell you, Aidan was thinking seriously one time of going to Vietnam? Yeah! I think he got the idea from me. I told him about the place, the Vietcong and all that. He didn't get around to going, though: too fond of the women. Will you look at him over there now beside Mam, and the old head of him? Queer impudent-looking, ain't he? Sideways, from here, he looks the spit of the old lad.

Ah, but this place would give you the shivers. And all the queer coons that've turned up: never thought I knew so many people in all my life. Listen, Brudgie! I'll talk to you again. I see someone I want to have a word with down here.

Ah damn it, that Brudgie one might as well be up there on the pedestals with them statues, for all the good you'd get from chatting to her. And the long face of her: you'd think it was her funeral Mass. Put a white veil over her head and chalk on her cheeks and you really could put her up there with the statues. Air hostess, how are you – a nun is what that one'll be, and then no fellow will ever get his shagging paws on her. But I'm off down here to see someone else. Oh now, things *are* starting to look up.

Well, hello, Minnie, tut tut tut . . . Fancy seeing you here. How are the fellows treating you lately, Minnie? That's some strong scent you're wearing there; lovely though. What's it called? No, don't tell me, let me guess. Apple Blossom, is it? Bet you now I'm right, aren't I?

Remember the Sunday in the shop when you were talking to the queer one? There was no need to be so worried: I'd never have said anything to Aidan. Very funny, though, you running out of the shop after me, and all steamed up like a Christmas pudding. What's this carry-on here, I says to myself. I thought you were going to ask me for a date or something. What's the world coming to at all, says I? Minnie must be taking to the chaps now. I must have looked a right gobshite, not having a clue about the tut tut tut . . . you know. But you weren't long about setting me straight now, were you?

14

I WAS NERVOUS GOING UP TO THE BACK DOOR OF THE priest's house that Friday evening, lest old Mrs Brennan or the priest himself came out. What if they had not gone to town at all that day? If either of them had appeared, I was going to say: Minnie's mother told me to give her a message. And if they'd asked what it was, I was going to say: She told me to be sure and give Minnie the message myself.

I was there a good ten minutes, about to go away, when Minnie opened the door. Come on in, hon, says she; nobody'll eat you. They're all gone to town. She brought me into the kitchen, sat me down and made this whopper of a cheese sandwich for me, with lashings of tomato sauce.

What was on the agenda? Had she some book with pictures in it she was going to show me? Or snaps of herself and Aidan in action in someone's hayshed, which one of her giggly mates maybe had taken in a hide nearby. Wouldn't have put it past her: she was a queer hawk, that one. Half afraid, I was, of what was next after the sandwich. Then she says: I have an idea. Come on. So I followed her out the kitchen door and into the hallway leading to the front door. She turned at the bottom of the big stairs and headed on up. I was scared out of my wits by then, but I'd asked for it and I'd have to stick with it all the way.

Minnie was a couple of steps ahead of me, up the stairs. The calves of her legs were rounded. Not too rounded like a hurler's or anything, but rounded all the same; evenly so. I could see traces of heat diamonds that tailed back from her shins. Mam said it was only people who were always hogging the fire got them. A shame, I thought. They took away from the lines of her legs – the lines that curved upwards in front of my eyes, and just about made it under the cover of her pink mini before they ran out of leg altogether. The flower-patterned wrap-around apron, much as it tried, couldn't hide all this, and stretched back its folds to open out as she climbed the

stairs. A mystery, those curves, what they led to under
the mini, and the idea of the miniskirt itself: showing
so much, revealing nothing. All a shagging mystery.
And Minnie had the key of it.

Even the stairs, where they led to, were mysterious.
Everything was going bloody well up. I was nervous
and didn't know what to expect. The mixture of the
two – the expectation and the nerves – some strange
concoction, boy; it would go to your head. I thought
of Murphy's thoroughbreds standing at the gate, so
tetchy they used to scare off into a gallop at the least
noise. Exactly how I felt: ready to tear off out of there
at any sound other than the thuds of our steps on the
stairs carpet, the deep red plush carpet. The height of
luxury, that house! The very same carpet was on the
landing above. I followed her into a room.

It was sparse enough there in the big room, mind
you, compared to the rest of the house. No fancy
carpet on the floor, just polished floorboards and
a mat by the bed. A wooden-framed single bed,
nothing fancy, was over by the front window; a table
with a white crochet cloth, and a prayer book on top,
was against the landing wall with a smaller table
between it and the head of the bed. There was this
box-shaped, wood-veneered radiogram sitting on the

small table, and a pile of records on a shelf under-neath. Against the opposite wall stood a big baulk of a wardrobe.

Father Breen's bedroom? I said. Yes, says she, and now don't you go touching any of his stuff; he knows to the last inch where everything is. She looked around, making sure there was nothing out of place, then made straight for the radiogram. She bent down on her hunkers to look through the stack of records, picked one out, straightened her back, lifted the cover off the radiogram and put on the record. This is the best I can do, says she; he's not into the Stones, the Beatles or any of that. He can't abide pop music.

I couldn't figure out her saying that this was the best she could do – I hadn't asked her to put on any records. I wasn't saying no to it, though. The novelty of it! Everything she did was just fascinating. After all, it was only a bit of information I'd asked her for. I hadn't expected to be given a grand tour of the curate's house, or brought on a pilgrimage to his bedroom.

Damn it! Bedrooms were private, sacred places, like the graveyard beyond or inside the chapel. On top of that, there was the dread of Father Breen walking in any minute and catching us. It was all right for her: she worked there. But what would I say when he'd ask: Hey, son, what do you think you're doing inside my bedroom?

There was this woeful farty noise, then an orchestra came on: some old waltz thing. Minnie turned up the sound. I'd heard it before, I wasn't sure where, probably on Radio Eireann's *Hospitals' Request* in the middle of the day of a Wednesday. I could never be bothered with that stuff, not till now anyway. I looked in over her shoulder. The name on the record cover read *The Blue Danube*, a long tail out of one of the letters going off in the shape of a bendy river. Will the priest mind you doing this? I asked. Oh, what he won't know won't bother him, says she. She said it like she owned the place.

That was the first time I'd ever heard a record on a real live player. Sound filled the room: rich, brown and bright, flowing like the river from the letter on the cover. A sparkling thing filled, flowed and changed the place to magic, like that time way back, in the kitchen at home, when I went in from the dark to find Aidan dancing with the brush. I was filled with the very same feeling. The moment was back again after all the years in between. Fresh as a daisy;

as if there were no years in between, really, and the two moments were one and the same, and there was nothing else, no other moment ever in the world, nor ever would be, but this instant going on and on.

Freedom again; yeah freedom, like the freedom-bubble sensation of sitting in the trailer behind the tractor going to the mill with Aidan, only this was much stronger. There was nothing imaginary about it, this was the real thing and no old brush stuck down in a bucket for an excuse either. Right before my eyes, the real Minnie took off twirling and waltzing round the floor, with a swish and a sway to her hips. Raised ankles caught the evening sunlight stealing in through the lace curtain that matched the crochet tablecloth. One arm was cocked out sideways, and the other sloped up in front of her with the palm of her hand cupped down. I copped on: she was dancing with an invisible partner. Next thing, herself and the invisible man waltzed over to me. Ah, this was class, boy.

She curtsied and bowed before me, like I was the blooming Queen of England. Next dance please, says she. How can anyone dance that old stuff? says I, not meaning a bit of it. It isn't modern, the twist, the hucklebuck or anything; only old two-stepping stuff that went out long ago with the fairies and the silent movies. I made a face, letting on to be disappointed in her knowing how to dance that way, and that it didn't suit the Minnie I knew to be out of fashion. Now if it was a pop song, says I, I'd show you one or two flashy moves all right, but this stuff! She knew I was only cod-acting, that I wasn't disappointed or anything; that the face, and the gab, were only an excuse for not knowing how to dance. And the big grin of her: *she* knew the story all right.

Come on, says she; I'll show you, and she dragged me out of my stupor of being fixed to the floor. Count, says she: WAN two three, WAN two three, WAN two three. And away we went, off clod-hopping like we were in training for a three-legged race – feet tied frontways instead of sideways. It was the best I could do: not to plant my crubeens on top of hers, or worse still to fall over her, knock her head against the wardrobe and brain her altogether. Useless, says she then, useless. Let us try it another way with you. Who's the *us*? There's only me and you here, not a frigging busload from Dublin, I was on the point of asking her.

Was there more than one person or what, inside that one's head? It wouldn't have surprised me a bit;

nothing about her would have. Look't here, says she, all you have to do is follow my feet around. Surely that's not too much for you? She went walking backwards, slowly, and I sent my feet after her, one foot after the other. Simple. We were – I mean I was – beginning to move to the music. I started to burst with laughing, but I was laughing from embarrassment. I didn't know if she knew that.

The tune ended. She broke off to go set the record playing again, came back and we motored around the bedroom together. This must be the queerest sight of all time, I thought. Not that bad now after all, is it? says she. The bumps on her chest moved in nearer to me.

What age are you now? she asked. Forty-five next birthday, says I back real quick, so as she wouldn't push to know. She tittered. You're old enough anyway, she said. There was going to be no big deal about age around there, and I could get the whiff of scent off her as we moved up close. What's the make of that perfume? says I, trying to fix my mind on to something – anything. She sort of bent her head and whispered to me: Apple Blossom. Why, do you like it? Like it! Does a cat sup milk?

Then her head was against mine, and mine was

starting to whirr at the touch. I felt the heat in my body drawing me close to her, or her to me, didn't know which. Everything was so warm, so pleasant – pleasant, like the dreams I'd had sometimes, lately. Like opening the door to a strange room; a room of soft amber light, plush rose-velvet covering every-thing and a red pile carpet two feet deep on the floor you could drop down into and roll around on for ever, and the smell of Apple Blossom. Yeah, a dream all right. I was dreaming about something that was actually happening, both at the same time.

But then didn't this fellow in my head shout: Wake up, wake up! And start complaining to the rest of me: Hey, you *cábóg*, you're way out of your depth here, you know that; not in control of yourself at all. Is this what you came here for? It was like there was two of me, one saying one thing, the other wanting the opposite. She's dictating everything that's happening here. Take control of yourself; let her know you're your own boss and stop clowning about, the lad in my head went on.

And stop I did. I pulled back from her, from the comfort. I tried to catch her eye, so she'd know what I meant and I wouldn't have to spell it out. But Minnie wasn't looking. She was off thinking of something else, like none of this amounted to much for her. I knew, all too bloody well, it didn't; that she was used to this caper and more, and everything – whatever everything was. To her, it was only like sitting down to a cup of tea, saying to herself: Will I or won't I have a chocolate biscuit along with it, or maybe a piece of sweet cake instead?

We danced on till the tune played out. But there was space between us again, good safe breathing space. My head was saying: Good man yourself. At last you're back in charge of things, not before time, so keep it this way. That was only my head though. The rest of me craved to be back in where the heat was, to be in close to her; as if she was pulling me in with an invisible grappling hook.

Grappling hooks! Suddenly I was reminded of the cat's limp body being pulled from the draw-well. I felt a shiver: there was a strange link, somehow, between us here in the room, grappling hooks and dead bodies. Was that thing that happened between a man and woman linked up to things dead? At that moment, I was sure it was.

She took off the record and was sliding it back in its cover when the doorbell rang: a loud clattering ring below in the hallway. She saw I was ready to

panic, but only laughed. Didn't you ask me something last Sunday? says she. Yeah, I did, says I. Now
look't here, if you want answers, do what I tell you,
says she. Do you want your question answered? The
doorbell clattered again. Yeah, OK, I said, getting
agitated. Yeah.

Here you go so, says she. She opened the wardrobe,
pointed to the inside and said: In you go. Come on
quick; I've to answer the door. Hah? says I, giving
her a queer look. Hurry, will you? Come on quick,
says she, ignoring my objections. Another ring at the
door. Ah, what the hell, I said. In I went to the
wardrobe; in among the wooden hangers, hooks –
hooks again – and black suits. Now leave the door
open just a little bit, like this, and don't make a
sound, do you hear? says she, and closed me in.
She went over to the bed: Can you see me all right
from here? Yeah, I said, wishing she'd get on and
answer the door. I could see the whole bed, the
window over it and the lace curtain. What was it
about that lace curtain? I was trying to remember
but couldn't, and it grigged me. Yeah, at last, I had it:
the lace of the curtain matched the crochet cloth
under the prayer book on the table. Was that all
it was?

Though the table was out of sight, I had a picture of it fixed in my head along with raised heels in sunlight, trip-stepping on the floorboards. The sound of the blue bendy-river tune was still beating around in my ears. Funny what goes on in the head while you're waiting for something to happen.

For a moment I felt safe in among the suits and shirts but, like running under the table in thunder when I'd been a chiseller, it wasn't safe at all. If Father Breen wanted a suit, all he'd have to do was come and open the wardrobe. Some look, though, he'd have on his face then: two whites of eyes glaring out at him, like a cat in the dark. What would I do? Run, what else. I'd jump out and run like a hoor, fast as ever the legs would carry me. A shirt there thrown over my head, or a black coat, so he wouldn't know what kind of creature was flying out past him. Supposing it was Mrs Brennan looking for that very shirt to iron, only to find it on legs meeting her, heading out the wardrobe door? No fear that that old one would fall back on the hump of her arse, kick up her clogs and die of fright. Tough as a badger, she'd probably take off after me, like she does when she tears out through the stones to ring the church bell. Aye, all very funny, ain't it? I was thinking. But it was not a bloody bit funny, and the sweat was out through me.

Whoever it was was inside now. I could hear the muffled voices away at the bottom of the stairs. Next they were coming up the stairs. Oh shite! Opening the door, and then they were in the room. Oh hell, what would I do? Hide behind the suits and shirts? I couldn't do that: I'd only make a noise. So I froze.

Minnie was doing all the talking, giggling away like the ones in school. I knew that voice. It was Aidan! What the feck was he doing there, and why wasn't he at home working for the old lad? He must have come up to the shop and then called over to see Minnie, knowing she'd be on her own this time of a Friday. No, there was more to it than that: Minnie had asked me if I'd wanted answers, had told me what to do and checked that the door was open enough. She knew what she was doing; she must have had it all planned. Well, bloody hell!

The caper started. I didn't see anything at first. I only heard it: the slurp, suck, smacking stuff. You'd think it was Vronnie Byrne eating a leg of chicken – the big toothless fish lips sucking every last scrap of meat off the bone, round and round, then the marrow, like it was never going to end. Suck slurp. The way you'd smack-lick an ice-pop, making it last. It's all right doing it yourself, but pure torture having to listen to someone else.

Then the cooing started up, the wood-pigeon cooing. Minnie was doing a bit of giggling, then she said: Don't be naughty, Aidan. Will you take it easy, for feck sake. (Aidan taking things easy? That was a laugh.) Slow down, will you. You're not on the tractor now, she says.

Aidan steered her backwards towards the bed, and into view. Like the pictures coming on in the hall: one minute nothing, the next a perfect picture. All that was missing was the lead-in: the flashing numbers, crosses and credits. Minnie slumped back on to the bed and he was on top of her, a starved ape bending down over a food parcel, tearing away at the wrapping. Except it wasn't bits of paper, it was clothing that was flying off this parcel. Aidan stood up and unwrapped himself: shirt, trousers and working boots went flying everywhere. Naked as two jaybirds, they were then. Some sight. The funniest pair of birds you could imagine: all legs jangling, backs, arses and arms. I had to cover my eyes and bite my sleeve to keep from laughing, looking at Aidan's big sweaty rump thrashing back and forth, like the knuckle-joint on the winnowing machine.

The next thing it was all over. All that was left were two hunks of fleshy carcasses lying there on the bed, still as dead meat. It was like a shotgun had been fired – bang, bang – and blasted their lives away.

Get up from me, you big baulk, says she then, before you choke the living daylights out of me altogether. She said it like she was really browned off with him. I didn't understand the sudden change in her humour.

Bits of underwear were dragged back up, clothes put back on, boots tied and shoes slid into. Yeah, everything was parcelled back neat and tidy, all the apelike frenzy of earlier was finished. Not another word. It felt kind of sad the way they were. And what was all the big mystery?

They went downstairs and she let him out the back door. I stayed inside the wardrobe, with my thoughts. I was glad the big lump of naked ape had gone. Doing what he did to her! It was like something she'd had no say over, or didn't know how to have a say in; that this was the expected, the done thing, and she'd been helpless. But this wasn't true either. If Minnie was anything, the one thing she wasn't was helpless. She had her own mind, I knew that much about her at least. It didn't seem, though, that what'd happened on the bed with Aidan was quite what she'd wanted. Why then had she gone along with it? That was the real mystery.

She was disappointed in him, I could tell, and I didn't blame her. I mean, he'd hardly strung two words together. He didn't say: How's it going, Minnie, since the last time I saw you, or anything. Nothing, just suck suck, then back on to the bed in a flash, and bang bang. Talk about Flash Gordon. Flash bloody Aidan, boy, the fastest gun in the West.

Could that have been the way the thing worked, how the job operated, when men and women went out courting? Maybe there wasn't any other way. Then I thought of powder-puff Rourke, herself and Patsy Doran: the way they'd been when me and Mikey had seen them the Sunday before. A different caper altogether.

I hardly noticed Minnie coming back and opening the wardrobe door. Strange, one minute everything was dark, the next light came flooding in. I put my hand up to my eyes. Her hands were against her cheeks, head bent, as she looked in at me. She was waiting for my reaction. The very same face as little Jimmy used to have when he was a toddler inside in the playpen, after flinging his rattle away from him; the mouth turned down at the sides, as much as to say: was I bold, have I overstepped the mark, or what? Then she burst out laughing. I laughed with her and stepped out of the wardrobe.

But her laughing was turning to crying, and then she bawled altogether. I put an arm around her and gently pulled her head down on to my shoulder. I felt for her, like I felt for Jimmy when he used go roaring-bawling after falling and cutting himself, and needed someone just to comfort him.

She was getting better. She turned her head sideways and looked up at me through sheepish, watery eyes. Was that educating enough for you? says she, through the end of the sobs, keeping the eyes fixed on me till she got an answer. So I squeezed her shoulder and said: You know, you didn't have to go to all that trouble on my account. Oh, no trouble, says she. Then she lifted her head and laughed. No trouble at all.

The next thing she grabbed my shoulders: Listen, you'd better get to hell out of here before they come back, or you'll end up spending the night inside the wardrobe.

Are you shagging codding me or what? says I. We both burst our sides laughing at the good of it, and tore away down the stairs. I was heading out the door I came in when she said: Listen, do you really want to learn how to dance? Yeah, sure, I said. OK then, call again the same time next Friday so. I will, says I. Like hell I will, I says in my own mind.

I was heading over the street when the priest's black Volkswagen Beetle came tut tut tuttering along nice and easy. A close shave that. Himself and Mrs Brennan sat in front; the handles of two shopping baskets perched up on the back seat. Everything was properly wrapped in brown paper and corded.

I was thinking of the shopkeepers and clerks in their white and brown coats: all clean, neat and exact, but not too exact; still friendly. Yes, Mrs Brennan, indeed, Mrs Brennan, and what kind of biscuits would his reverence prefer this week? The butcher too, forefinger pointing back to the red raw carcass, which looked like Aidan's arse, hanging from the hook, telling her: We have this special piece of steak here, just right for you. Oh let me assure you it's been properly hung. Wouldn't dream of offering it to you otherwise. No doubt about it, those shop assistants knew their job and how to treat people. I began thinking of parcels and food. Nothing else mattered as I headed for home.

15

THE LAST TIME I FELT ANYTHING FOR THE OLD LAD WAS the time of the gun trouble with Patsy Doran. I'd never liked shotguns since Aidan pointed one at me. A shotgun, how are you! That rusty double-barrel excuse for one must've been at least a hundred years old; could backfire or anything. He did it for the lark, shouting: Bang bang, you're dead! The old lad swiped it right out of his hands and warned him never to point a gun at anyone, even when it wasn't loaded. I knew then that guns were nasty, and the more I saw of them, the more I disliked them.

Watching the old lad or Aidan carrying it, heading out to shoot crows and rabbits, would put the heart crossways in you. I used to imagine all sorts of dreadful accidents happening till he'd get back, and I'd relax again only on seeing the stock being broken and each piece hung up separately on nails under the kitchen ceiling. Although put away, the gun still held a certain menace about it.

Patsy Doran had an acre of ground at the back of his house, just this side of the village. He was the greatest man of all time for vegetables: cabbages, carrots, lettuces, onion sets – you name it, he'd have it there. Twice a week at least he'd hitch the trailer to the back of the Anglia, tie on the creels and load up for town. Vronnie Byrne said he made more in one summer flogging scraps of leaves than he earned all year round clerking above for Murphy's. He'd live in your ear, that fellow, is what she said, and she'd know. When he wasn't behind the counter, he was out there stuck in the middle of the plot, himself and the scarecrow. Sometimes you wouldn't know which was which.

You've a mighty fine crop there this year altogether, Patsy, somebody would say. You'd see the nostrils twitch out with pride, like sails in the wind – some bulb of a nose for the size of the little head on him. How come you always have them so good,

Patsy? they'd say, just to wind him up, like. The head would cock back, the nose fill out and away he'd go in a hack: 'Tis the sheep's droppings that does it, the greatest fertilizer of all time. Liquid manure's your only man for the vegetables.

I often spotted him, with a bucket and shovel, going around the fields collecting sheepshit to mix with water. He kept that concoction in an old stone trough at the back of the house. Some whiff, I tell you, when he stirred it up of a hot summer's day. Imagine, he'd go in behind the counter then, sticking his paws down sweet jars and counting out slices of ham.

Sometimes he used to ask me, all smiley big teeth and with no one else in the shop: I say, what field are your sheep in now? Of all the sheep I know, yours are the ones that make the best droppings; I say, the best droppings. I never knew what way to take him: was he in earnest or only jeering? You'd be inclined to say something back: feck off, and mind your own business. But it was better to say nothing, in case he'd dish you out the wrong change or charge you too much when you weren't minding.

I'd grown even more wary since Vronnie told me the carry-on with him and the old lad over Mrs

Rourke. I felt awkward facing him, knowing the story, and especially with no one else there serving. The last thing you'd want was to get drawn into a conversation about sheep's droppings. It was torture having to ask him for the items of shopping. I'd try to say as little as possible: a pound of butter, half-pound of tea, pound of sugar and a large tin of beans, the biggest size – there, on this side of the shelf – please. A sort of please-and-thank-you job. I'd pay up and grab the change: Thanks, have to go now, 'bye. Then out the door like a bullet I'd go before he'd start prating.

That didn't always work, though. The times Doran'd have nothing else to do, only stare out the window at passers-by, and he'd spot you coming over the street. Open the shop door – jing a ling – and there he'd be, leaning out over the counter as if he was seven feet tall, hands joined like a holy man praying for mankind, or some strange breed of cross-eyed cat crouching, ready to spring from the top of the counter and pounce on its prey. He was cross-eyed because of the glass eye, after the time the old lad hit him with the hurl. You never knew rightly whether he was looking at you or staring out the window watching somebody else. You could take it he'd noticed you only when a gap-toothed grin flashed across his face. Even then you couldn't be sure.

I was never sure either whether it was the usual shopkeeper's grin he had on, or if he was just stripping his teeth at the sight of a Cullen – any Cullen. A mongrel dog, after all the years of remembering and crouching in wait, was snarling and ready to bite back. Well, how are you today, young Cullen? he'd say, rubbing his palms. You just knew he was sizing you up – measuring the victim who had fallen within his grasp.

Like the time he started, in that drawl of his, calling out my list of shopping before I'd even got to open my beak. The usual half-pound of tea is it? says he. Then in a litany: the pound of butter, the pound of sugar and the tin of beans. Oh I nearly forgot, the biggest tin isn't it – on this side? Big into the beans, aren't we, in your house? It must get a bit windy there though, by times, does it? Ha ha ha. I say, does it get windy in your house?

I felt the hair stand on the back of my neck, like you would watching the Hunchback of Notre Dame in that horror film. Windy ha ha, how are you! He hadn't a clue how to go about being a jeer; he didn't even get it half right. You could do with a few lessons from Red Bill, you shitehawk you, was on the tip of my tongue. But what I said was: Red Bill's the only man for saying things like that. It came out arseways. He picked up on it though, and didn't like it. The face went stiff. I think he was careful with me after that; at least, he didn't jeer as much.

Other times, he'd be all over you with niceness; asking, again with the palms rubbing: How is the boss-man at home this weather? Haven't seen him in ages. Keeping well, is he? The voice gentle as a whisper. I always felt a strange, extra mistrust of him asking me that, while knowing full well there was no love lost between them. I mean, what normal person would enquire after their enemy's well-being? But was that thing there a normal person? Or was it some alien creature, sticking out its long treacly tongue to wind round the back of your head, swipe you up like a wisp of straw, pull you into its slobbering mouth of gurgling gungy sweetness and on down the slimy gullet-cavern to its green gut; licking, the way a cow after calving rasp-licked the cleanings from its new-born.

He could let it be known, too, how he really felt towards our crowd. He was under pressure one day, with a clatter of customers waiting to be served. I was there for ages, going from one foot to the other, fidgeting with the handles of Mam's shopping bag and expecting – hoping – to get served next. But he ignored me and went on tending to the others, although they had come in after me. I'm next there in line to be served, says I, fed up of waiting. He didn't give me much soothe, though. If you're in such a big hurry, young Cullen, says he, why don't you go some-place else for your few bits?

It was the *few bits* that got me. I did just that: turned on my heels, marched off out with myself – it felt good – and went over to the corner shop.

Not that that was such a hot idea either. The old one in there stocked little or nothing: pens, envelopes, school copies and that kind of stuff. A few other items, maybe: sugar, tea, a bit of sweet cake, cans of bull's-eyes and hard sweets – hard as rocks to break your teeth on, like she intended breaking the last tooth of every hoor in the country. Of course she had tins of beans, but no ham, butter, cheese or fruit. On the high shelves loaves of bread – stale bread – were spread out lengthways, giving the impression of more there than there was.

Sure you know very well I have no cheese, says she to me once. Why can't you go where you always go, and don't be bothering me when you know I haven't got these things? Another time I asked for bread soda. Bread soda? So now he expects me to stock bread soda, does he? He'll be asking me to keep motor cars next. Take the face off you, she would. And she was nosy. What's this for? What's that for? Is that right now? What do you want it for anyway? To frigging eat, missus, what do you think? To fly to the flipping moon? She'd hear you, too, muttering under your breath, and she'd ask: What's that you're saying there about me now?

You'd kind of like her, though, in spite of herself. She was straight out with things, a bit like Vronnie Byrne that way, and she'd never do you on the change. If she'd stocked even most of what I'd wanted, on them old bockety shelves, I'd never once have darkened the door to that other fellow. Didn't relish the thought one bit, then, of having to face back into Murphy's the time after that.

Ah, Mr Cullen's back is he? says your man; I knew it wouldn't be long till he'd be over again to see how we're all getting on here. The smirk of him and the gaps in his teeth, or was it the fangs he was stripping. And for some reason, I started thinking of

Mrs Rourke. Yeah, it's the fangs, I says to myself; them fangs.

I felt sorry for the woman. Poor Mrs Rourke. So that was why she'd always looked so pale and gaunt and had to plaster up her face like. There in bed together, after sailing up and down them seven seas all evening, he'd start to feel peckish. So what would he do? Only grab her round the back of the head with that long tentacle tongue of his, sink the fangs into her neck and suck out the blood. Mr Dracula Doran himself – that's who was really standing there behind the counter. He sucked blood from people: to drink, or mix with sheep's droppings to feed big hungry vegetables to flog to the townies. Ah, that was it for sure, the secret formula of his vegetables.

Imagine the shopkeepers and townies hearing that news: It's not fresh vegetables at all yous are eating, but sucked blood and sheepshit mixed up in a rusty bucket. Now, townies, what do you say to that? Anyway, how would a townie know a vegetable, except for, maybe, when it was before him on the table. Poor old Rourkie below would lie there, drained; not enough strength left either to toss Captain Bligh out of bed or bar him from the house altogether. Maybe she got mesmerized from looking into them slanty eyes of his, and came under his spell. Was that what was happening to Minnie? Did she fall under a spell any time Aidan appeared over the horizon?

It was the first time I'd ever thought of those two women as having anything in common. That being the case, there was bound to be a link between Aidan and that blood-sucking Drac who stood before me. I wondered was it some strange power of mesmerizing women they both had; a sort of a demon thing? And was Aidan serving his time as some kind of an apprentice demon?

Yes, says he, what can I get you? The smirk was gone from the face, and the mouth was moving. Yes, says he again, what is it you want? Something in my head was telling me it was about the fourth time he'd asked me that. Wake up, I told myself. A pound of what? says he. A pound of blood and sheepsh— Sorry – butter, a pound of butter, says I. Butter wasn't on the list, it just came out of my mouth. But, not wanting to make a bigger spectacle of myself, I left it at that. He looked at me queer.

Mr Fing Fang Drac stood gawping, and waited for me to call out the rest of my messages, so he could move on to serve the two customers there after me. Things were improving in the place.

Mogue Doyle

The trouble started when our sheep broke into his plot of vegetables. As luck would have it, the only outfield we have, away from the rest of the land, happens to be stuck right beside his house. At home it's known as *the street field* because it's near the village. Aidan said: Doran tried to buy it off our crowd once when we were on good terms, and it would have been sold to him too, probably, but for the row; no fear of him ever getting his greedy paws on it now though. Doran robs all the fencing I put on the ditch to keep the sheep in, and uses it for firing because he's too mean to buy coal. Sure I saw him doing it. That's what Aidan said. When was this? asks the old lad. Sure it was only about a week or so ago, the last time I saw him. He's always in our field gathering dung, says Aidan. Sure he'd have to be making gaps, going in and out like that.

And would you ever think of telling him to stop? the old lad asked. No flies on Aidan though: Sure I often tried to tell him, but the minute he sees me coming he's gone like a light. He had an answer for everything.

It was Mikey who brought the message, on his way home from the street. I was passing the house, says he, when Patsy Doran ran out to call me back. The man could hardly speak, and frothing out of the mouth he was. Go in and tell that fucking shower of Cullens to get themselves up here quick, and take their hooring hungry sheep off my property fast as ever they can, or I'll take the gun to every last one of them. His very words, says Mikey. Mikey himself was frothing telling us. His voice was shaking, repeating Doran, word for word, up to the old lad's face.

I was afraid your man would shoot every last sheep in the field, and that the old lad might go berserk and murder him for it. You couldn't trust something like that wouldn't happen. Two ruthless boyos, each with a dangerous streak, who wouldn't think twice about dragging us all with them over the edge to destruction. Storm clouds were gathering in the head. The dots of grey mist were back again too, except they weren't grey now; they were turning to streaks of black, like black rain. Shadows of fear, anger or hatred, or a mixture of them all, crowded out everything else.

I knew that this thing in my head, bad and all as it was in itself, was no more than a sign for something else – so great a disturbance I couldn't dare even imagine it. Whatever it was, it had to be the worst

207

possible thing in all creation, seeing as the thing I used to imagine to be the worst was now, itself, only the sign for it.

Aidan and the old lad got the dog and made off up the yard. You better come too, the old lad roared back at me. You might be of some use to us. Some fecking use you are yourself, you shagging old hog, says I. What did you say? he roared back at me. I said that you'll definitely need the sheepdog, says I. The two of them walked up that road like demons at dusk: grim black shapes of determined bastards on a mission to a place of the worst kind of horror, the place of the damned. And it showed in their speed: they walked like the clappers of hell. There was no point trying to catch up with them. I had too much lead in my step, whereas their legs seemed to get lighter till they were almost dancing, way up ahead. They'd turned into dangerous, jigging, dancing shapes on their way to a rendezvous, to do battle with another black shape and see who'd become the blackest, the lord of black shapes. I'd seen it in the pictures.

It had to be, I heard myself saying to the ditch beside me, one of those cases where perfectly normal men during daylight hours grow out of their skins and change into beasts the minute the sun goes down

– desperate marauding beasts that go off prowling, and stalking their prey, innocent or otherwise. Same as it'd said in the pictures, and that was supposed to have been all make-believe. But it wasn't make-believe, was it? No, a lot of it was based on true stories. Nobody could ever dream up such stuff.

As anyone could tell you, truth was stranger than fiction. There was no need to concoct yarns when they were there to be had from real life. *Dracula* was supposed to have been just that: a yarn. But it wasn't a yarn. There was this tulip called Dracul back in history one time, in Romania or someplace. He used to put all his enemies – thousands upon thousands of them – on stakes along a roadside, like this roadside. It was far worse than in any pictures. Your man in the pictures only took bites out of young ones' necks; the real McCoy used to shove people's bodies down on to sharp-pointed stakes. Where was the comparison, like? You could understand the film-makers not wanting any fuss made about the truth, so as not to put people off going to see their films. Or maybe governments had forced them not to say anything, like, for fear of causing total chaos round the world.

So now my family had two tyrant monsters in it: one fully trained, the other one still only an apprentice. The distance between us grew till they were eventually out of sight. I was on my own, cut off from light and living things. I never thought I'd feel scared on a road I was so used to. Each house was different to the one I knew, or thought I knew, and no longer friendly or welcoming. Could it be they weren't houses at all? Only squat ghouls of things, their box-eyes glinting out, mouthing strange sounds in a strange lingo to mock people passing on the road. Maybe they said things I'd be better off not knowing anyway. I walked on, trying to keep my eyes straight in front of me. Except I couldn't stop them going off sideways to pick out creepy shadows. Every branch stirring in the breeze was an ogre reaching down.

At last I made it to the street field, and climbed the iron gate to see were the sheep lying dead: scattered, dead and bleeding, flat on the ground, like I'd expected. But they weren't at all. They were walking around contented, heads bent, chomping away on the grass in the last dregs of the day's dusk light. That was a relief. The only thing was, they weren't all there; you could tell without having to count them. I got down off the gate, went up to that house of doom next to the field and looked in over the garden wall.

Almost unreal, that's what it was. Three figures of

men – no, not men, they only looked like men; they were demons, as I'd expected – were standing in the front garden close to the house. They were nearly black against the light that raked out from the porch ceiling inside. The one nearest the house had his back to the door. I couldn't make out the expression on his face – the fangs of teeth, nose, or the slanty eyes that'd tell me for sure it was the Patsy Doran demon. I knew it was him, though: the smallest of the three, with the head too small for the rest of him.

There was this thing he was holding and pointing at the biggest of the three. I knew, only too well, what it was. He started roaring about the damage the sheep had done to his crop. He screamed at the big demon what he'd do to him. And the names: a bully, a bastard, a land-grabber . . . a maimer. As well he might, I allowed, holding that thing in his hands and pointing it.

The threats came spuming out of him for what seemed like ages. The big figure said nothing. He just stood there and took the abuse like it was his lot to take. I felt the horror in the pit of my stomach. I was scared for the old lad. I may not have liked him much, but I still didn't want to see him get shot. And he was close to that now. I couldn't move myself: it was as if I was rooted to the ground, or every last ounce of my energy had drained away. All I could manage was to slam the lids shut over my eyes and wait for it to happen: the bang, the bleeding, the beast's body shaking on the ground as his life slipped away. I'd seen animals put down, and their limbs twitched long after they were dead.

I expected it to end for definite, when the old lad pushed up close against the shotgun and said to Doran: Are you going to pull that fucking trigger or not? The calm way he said it – no shouting – mocked the fever of madness in the man with the gun, making little of it.

Stand back there or I'll let you have both barrels, Doran roared at him, and he gave a jerk, himself and his gun, backwards towards the house. A crouched type of jerk, as if the gun was another limb on his body and not a separate thing at all.

Well, go on – do it. You haven't the guts to, have you? the old lad roared back at him. A defying, awful roar, the voice suddenly full of contempt.

I'd heard that same shout once, a long time before, yet I recognized it straight away. The day he'd chased Mam up the yard with the slop bucket and shrieked at her. That same roar now struck a different fear in me to the fears from the rest of what was happening: sharper, deeper, and it brought back the old hate. For a second I found myself wishing the gun would go off: saw myself there in Doran's shoes, squeezing that trigger. I closed my eyes and waited for the bang, for it must surely come, maybe even a second bang. I was more prepared now. The only noise, though, was the buzzing in my ears. I waited, but nothing, nothing happened.

Was the storm easing? I knew it was when Patsy Doran jibbed. Go on, says he. Take your blasted sheep out of here.

So, the old lad was right: your man hadn't the guts to pull the trigger. All he'd had to do was squeeze that little piggy – the gun would've done the rest – but he couldn't. He held the gun pointed at the old lad's feet and said: You'll pay me for the damage. The old lad just stood there. I knew he thought he'd won.

Aidan was the first to break from the scene. He edged towards the entrance to the vegetable plot round the back of the house, where the rest of the sheep must have been. The sheepdog went after him. I hopped over the wall and followed them, glad to be getting away. The sheep were scattered and having a right time munching vegetables. We rounded them up with the dog, and hooshed them out through the gap they'd made coming in. Easy enough to find the spot: bits of tell-tale wool clung to briars around the gap, still fluffy white against the near-dark.

A right bastard that fellow, says Aidan. It's been hardly a fortnight since I fixed up this very same gap. I had my doubts though. Why would Doran have taken the fencing? It wasn't the time of year for fires. He would've wanted a good, tight fence there anyway to protect his vegetables. I knew the gap Aidan was fixing all right, whenever he was up that neck of the woods, and it had nothing to do with keeping sheep's rumps in one place, and everything to do with hoisting female rumps on to clergymen's beds. When the sheep were back in the field, we collected all the branches we could find in the dark, criss-crossed them in the gap and left it at that. The old lad never gave us a hand either.

Are you sure they're all out of there? says Doran, on our way back. He was still carrying the gun but it was hanging from under his arm, the barrel broken. The metal cap of a cartridge in the breech caught a glint from the porch ceiling, and shone like Christmas tinsel. Though more at ease, he still had that cock-on-the-dunghill look about him, and jigged from one leg to the other. Neither of us answered him; we looked straight ahead and walked past. He was getting back some of his own medicine. He'd lost his sting, like a weak ram the old lad had castrated one time so it wouldn't breed any more poor quality lambs. It went strutting around for ages afterwards still thinking it was connected to its equipment.

The old lad was on the road, waiting. He asked Aidan if he'd seen where they'd broken out. Aidan said he'd closed up the gap as best he could, but wouldn't guarantee they'd not break out someplace else before morning. We should drive them home with us as a precaution for the night, and he'd give the hedge a right good fencing first thing the next day.

The old lad said: No, come on, we'll leave them where they are. I'll take sheep from my field for no one, certainly not for the likes of him. I was glad. I didn't fancy driving sheep home in the dark. Then he said a queer thing: I don't want you fellows having anything more to do with that gazebo, do you hear me? Fair enough, says I.

It was the first time he'd included me in anything all night. What had I done to deserve his lordship's favour? Did he think I might suddenly want to go off colloguing with Mr Doran? For heaven's sake! The old lad went on: Payment, he wants to be paid for the damage done. Huh! I'll give that geezer payment all right for pointing a gun at me. I'll pay him for that. It was a threat, and Sniggers Cullen didn't make idle threats: Patsy Doran would get paid for that evening. The thing wasn't over.

The next day in school, Mikey wouldn't stop asking me what'd happened. I was fit to give him a dig and make him shut up: none of his blasted business. I just said: Ah, no big deal really, we put the sheep back in the field and that was it. But it *was* a big deal. I couldn't stop wondering how Aidan was getting on at the fencing; was the old lad up there too, with the shotgun, and had there been a shoot-out? I thought of the threat.

Listening to Mooney, up at the map of Ireland on the board, was like a dream. His voice droned on: the name of this river, the name of that river and the counties they flowed through. Who gave a fiddler's feck where they flowed? The only river I knew was the one in the valley below. It wasn't on the map but was nonetheless real, like the night before had been real. The rivers on the map were only names. It was the same when Mooney changed on to the litany of mountains, just names until he came to the Blackstairs. Now that wasn't just a name; there was an actual mountain. I knew its shape. I'd climbed it and run down it. I'd felt its hard granite tear into my knees when I fell – you shagging arsehole of an anthill. It was there all right, the one genuine thing, for a change, you could both like and hate, and different from the things of the night before that you could only hate, like hating the names of unreal mountains and unreal rivers.

16

A COUPLE OF EVENINGS AFTER THAT, GOING HOME FROM school, me and Mikey were passing up by Rourke's. This figure of a man appeared in the shadows of the doorway for an instant, but then stepped back inside out of view – the way some fellow walking out too far on a cliff might suddenly stop, waver, find his balance and step back from the edge. For a second there I could've sworn it was the old lad. I knew it wasn't him though: what would he be doing there? None of our crowd ever went in hobnobbing with that one.

Hey, Mikey, who was that? I says, but he hadn't seen a sinner. Maybe my eyes were playing tricks, so I didn't give it another thought.

About a fortnight later, Mikey remarked to me: I

didn't know yous were friends with Mrs Rourke below. He said it real casual, the way you'd talk about some picture that was in the hall last night. But it wasn't casual; he'd only made it sound that way. He was fishing for information and hoped to catch me off guard, so that, like a telegraph machine in a Western, I might go tapping out some nice tidbit of ripe gossip he could fatten on. He'd be saying to himself: Well, well, what have we here now? What juicy bit of strange have I dug up to bring home? I'll tell the others and we can all have a right laugh, a right chew on it, over dinner.

Imagine them Cullens! The mess they've landed themselves in this time. Munch munch. Aren't they an awful shower too? Munch munch. Sure, what would you expect. Munch munch. Always in bother, that lot. Munch munch. That crowd! Munch munch. Landed themselves in the soup again, have they?

He'd get no free dinnertime's entertainment from me, or shagging tidbits on a plate; no Cullen for dinner for that day, I'd tell you. I decided to keep my answers plain and simple and as casual as his remark had been, like when he'd asked me about the episode with Patsy Doran and the sheep: I'd managed it well then. I'd do the same again. So I said: Ah sure, we were never bad friends with Mrs Rourke. We've often been in there from time to time – rambling, one thing and another. It's just, well . . . you didn't see us, you've never been there the same time as us – except the Sunday me and you went in. Remember that . . . aha, haa haa . . . I was stuffing him right well, as I thought.

Well, says he, I've seen your father in that house twice in the last few days, and how come I never saw him inside before?

He had me there. All I could say was: Oh, right. Twice within the last couple of days. *In there?* I tried to take it in, but the picture wouldn't focus right. I had no answer for him; no stuffing him this time. If it was cod-acting me he was, I'd break his head for him, the shagger.

But Mikey wasn't codding. Late home from school one evening shortly after, I was passing up by your one's house, and didn't the old lad come tearing out the gate like his arse was on fire. What had he been in there for? It had to be some business about land, stock, machinery or something like that. Could it be he was buying the Aga cooker? Mikey had said she was thinking of a new one.

More like, though, it had to do with the episode

over the sheep. He'd gone in to see Patsy Doran – often in there these days – or to leave a message for him. Mrs Rourke might even be acting as go-between: a referee laying down rules, keeping them talking, cajoling them, so they could sort out their row like civilized beings and not blow each other's head off with guns. Was that why he was there?

I could picture the two buckos sitting up at Mrs Rourke's big table in the back room. Now, gentlemen, she'd say, trying to appear cross through the lipstick and salmon-pink puff face, and looking in over their shoulders from out of the dark. Please sit up there and behave yourselves, and we'll have this little problem sorted out in next to no time. She'd give them tea and cake from her best bone china to sweeten them up, coax them along and get them to agree.

Agree on what though, I was wondering. What could those two ever agree on? Then I had it! The old lad was, after all, paying compo for the damage to the vegetables; the money Doran might make selling them, but wouldn't, because of our sheep. But they couldn't settle the amount. The old lad was keeping it down, while the other fellow was trying to get all he could. That's what it was, and they argued it out while sipping tea and sampling your one's sweet cake.

Oh now that'll do. Carrots, this summer, will make nothing near the colour of that kind of money. Cabbages have never been as plentiful in years. Don't take my word for it; anyone'll tell you that. More tea, Jimmy, hon? Go on, Jimmy, have another slice of cake, will you?

Nothing would get sorted out the first time. They'd leave off arguing when the cake ran out, but arrange to meet there again over tea in a few days. Several more goes like that, plenty of tea and sweet cake; eventually they'd come to some agreement and spit on their palms and shake hands to seal the bargain – the proper way, the way the cattle-jobbers did.

So that's what the old lad had been up to. That was why he was tearing off out the gate ahead of me, and kicking himself thinking about all the money he'd have to pay your man. More than likely, Doran was still inside. He'd hung on to an empty cup, letting on to be supping tea, so the old lad might finish first and take himself to hell out of the way. Then Doran and Mrs Rourke would hop into bed again, and away they'd swim the whole of the seven seas in the one blooming go. The wily hoor.

What are you doing coming home from school this hour? The old lad turned and quizzed me. Did you happen to see Owney Kearns on your way? Two questions at once. Which one did he want answered first? I had a choice. I knew he didn't give a curse what time I got home, or if I ever got home for that matter. He never asked about school; not unless I was in trouble and he'd have to face Mooney. No shortage of questions then. So, I allowed, I'd answer the one about being late first: just to be awkward. The master kept me back to clean up the corridor, says I – the first thing that came into my head. I didn't think he'd be interested in any school corridor!

Owney Kearns? he growled, before I could say another word. I asked you did you see Owney Kearns?

Who the hell is Owney Kearns? I wondered.

He was supposed to be in Rourke's this evening. He sent me word saying he'd meet me there. Did you see him, I'm asking you? He spluttered it at me, as if it was my shagging fault your man didn't turn up.

No, I didn't see him, says I. Something about it didn't sound right: the big deal he was making to me of a stranger not turning up to meet him. And why meet in Rourke's of all places? Was he supposed to have met him there the other times too? So it had been him in her doorway that evening, appearing like a shagging goblin – now you see him, now you don't – and not my eyes playing tricks.

Was he meeting Patsy Doran on the sly, and not wanting it to get around that he was paying compo, lest people might think he was gone soft in the head and an easy touch for other compo-gougers, licking their lips on hearing about it? The big deal about meeting that Kearns man might've been only a smokescreen; a yarn he'd concocted there and then for my benefit, in case I'd go mouthing out about having seen him.

Who the feck is Owney Kearns? I asked Aidan, bumping into him later outside the front door.

Never heard of him. Why? says he.

Every time you'd ask that loodheramaun a question, he'd have to ask you one back – himself and his *why*. Normally I'd have said: no why. But that time I wanted to draw him out and see what he knew, so I told him about the big meeting in Rourke's, the Kearns fellow not turning up and how the old lad was bucking over it.

Aidan landed his big fist on my shoulder and

steered me up the yard away from the front door. I lifted my elbow to puck him off but he didn't let go his grip, so I let fly with my foot. But he saw it coming and dodged back. Oh yeah? says he with the eyebrows flying up on the forehead like Groucho Marx.

What the hell's the matter with you? says I.

Now you listen here to me, he growled. You know, only this very day Mam was asking me if I'd seen himself going into Rourke's any time lately. He wagged his finger at me and looked around him at the same time. Trying to keep his voice down, he said: So, you, keep your big gob shut, and don't you go saying a word of any of this to Mam.

Why's that? says I.

Why do you think? he snapped. Because she'd only get upset, that's why. He was glancing around him again. Look't here, I don't know if you know this, says he then, and launched off into the yarn about the old lad and Mrs Rourke going out courting long ago. You know, going out, says he; going out like . . . like me and Minnie Brien. Full of frigging information, he was.

Oh yeah, says I, trying to wiggle the eyebrows, mocking him – except I hadn't the hang of it – and keeping in the guffaws. What did he take me for anyway? Was I supposed to think his *going out* with Minnie meant only a little hand-holding, some gentle pigeon-cooing on a park bench, a sky full of twinkly stars and a big fat moon gawping in over their shoulders. Some tender finger-touching, maybe: folderol lol, *I am yours and you are mine* sort of stuff – Mam's favourites. Mam would never again have to wait till she'd go to the pictures to see any of that. We suddenly had our own Mr Nelson frigging Eddy, flitting around with his Jeanette MacDonald. Nelson Eddy my arse! Nelson up-on-the-bed bang bang Aidan, more like. I was on to him on that score.

Aidan's voice changed: Now don't tell Mam, mind. She'd only get upset and think up all sorts of queer things about him, that he's back seeing that old hay-bag again on the quiet maybe. So say nothing.

I said I wouldn't. He was almost pleading with me to protect Mam, and I liked that about him. A side of him I'd not noticed much before.

Heaven knows, Mam needed protecting. She wasn't her old self any more: always withdrawn to that secret world of hers. You'd know she wasn't with you, from the glazed look when you'd say something, and she'd go huh – not having heard a word. The brown eyes that used to sparkle weren't there; the eye-holes were more sunken in the head, and the brown was gone as dull as wet clay. She said herself she thought she was getting cataracts, that things weren't as clear as they used to be.

Isn't that a blooming nuisance? says she, annoyed with herself as she handed me over the needle and spool. I can't even thread the darning needle. God bless your eyesight, son, says she; and always take care of them precious eyes, won't you? I'll have to get myself new glasses. She rested a hand on my head. The glasses she had she never wore anyway, except for squinting at papers and the *Woman's Own*. Anything to do with the royal family – especially Princess Margaret and your man, Snowdon – she'd read over and over, moving their pictures out from her, and going ahhh . . . She loved gawking at the fashions, cutting out designs for dresses, holding them up against the light in the window. Sometimes she'd smile. You wished you knew what made her smile.

Her hair was gone a mousy grey, and while she still tied it up in a bun at the back, it had lost its bounce. It was more stalky, coarsely tangled and no longer flowing from her head the way I liked to remember. I sometimes thought that if we could only turn back

the clock to the point when things had started to go wrong in our house, to where we'd veered off the right road, we would be able to have her back the way she'd been before. We could all start off again and maybe take the road right the next time.

Another thing about Mam: you'd never see a laugh out of her any more; she had no giggling fun. Not like the old nights of the gatchying inside in their room; the way they used to keep a body awake for ages carrying on, and making up after rows they'd had earlier.

Sometimes though, in my sleep, I'd hear him calling her in a low voice: Annie . . . Hey, Annie, are you awake? Are you awake, Annie? Will you come on over in here to me, Annie? But then I'd waken with a start – almost sitting up in bed – thinking what was this: were we back again to the old days? But all it ever was, was one of them stark dreams where everything's so clear and alive you remember it afterwards like it was real. She wasn't even in the same room as him any more at night. Little Jimmy was inside in her corner now. Only a few weeks previous, Mam had moved, bed and all, into Ciss's poky little room at the head of the stairs – after another big blow-up. Me and Aidan were still in the same old spot.

Of all the changes to Mam, the thing I missed most was the fun; it would do you good just to hear her laugh.

Standing there with Aidan in the middle of the yard, I reckoned that he too must have had feelings like these. I hoped not, though. He had no right to be down in the dumps; it wasn't in his nature, like. He was the one who did things, not the one who brooded over them.

I said: No no, it wasn't that at all; he was inside in Rourke's on business.

Aidan looked at me sideways, and made a face as much as to say: who do you think you're codding? You just make sure not to say a word to Mam, says he again.

I said no more. I didn't tell him how I thought the old lad might've gone in to Rourke's to meet Patsy Doran over the business of the sheep, the compo and all that. I couldn't, just in case he'd make a shite of that idea too.

17

LAST SUNDAY MORNING CAME WET. SOFT, BRIGHT summer rain sparkled down on a skew. There's nothing to beat this sort of rain for freshness; it seeps into everything and turns any of the crops that might be wilting a deeper shade of green. You could almost hear the grass grow.

It would take up – it was only a shower – and the match above in the field, in the afternoon, wouldn't be called off. Great. I'd have a few pucks of the ball with Mikey and Willy along the sideline and keep one eye on the game. Peter and the old lads would be there trying to best each other with yarns. Red Bill would give the team the shots as usual, letting rip with that razor-edge tongue of his. And Minnie would be there with her skewbaldy friends, eyeing up fellows in togs and tittering behind their hands at lads with bandy legs. I'd have to think up something to tell Minnie when I'd bump into her: why I hadn't bothered to call for another dancing lesson. Dancing lessons, my foot! Freddie Astaire you'd want to be to keep up with that one. I couldn't think offhand of a good excuse for her. Something, no doubt, would come to me during the day.

The only thing I wasn't looking forward to was Mikey asking questions about the old lad going into Rourke's and dragging that ass-load of scald back up again. I wanted to forget about all that. This was a new day, and what was called for was a brand new start to everything. I thought about the rain easing off, the sun breaking through the clouds and the greyness getting scattered away out of the sky. It was going to be a good day. But that's not what happened. The day failed, the sun didn't come out and the sky didn't clear.

Everything was normal enough, though, till dinnertime. The old lad ate up his dinner fairly quickly, and then disappeared. Full of beans he was too: up from the chair and out the door like he was a young lad again back in training. Indeed, the local team could do with his services nowadays, if what Peter had said about him was anything to go on. But all that rush wasn't quite his usual style for dinner-time of a Sunday. He liked to sit, after everyone else was gone, sipping tea and staring into a folded newspaper, in silence. This Sunday was different: he could hardly wait to finish up and get out; no cup of tea wanted.

Mikey appeared at the front door, tapping a ball on the hurl to let me know he was waiting. As usual, Ciss's eyes lit up when she saw him; you'd imagine she'd have known better by now. After the grub, we moseyed on down the road, tapping the ball to each other. I was behind, and Mikey was ahead facing me. I noticed he was going slower than usual. He's after downing too many spuds for dinner, I reckoned, or else something's on his mind.

What's wrong with you today, you lazy git? Will you move on out of that or we'll be late for the match, says I.

We were well past Rourke's below when he stopped, came up to me and said: Listen, I think I might have something to show you.

What the hell are you on about? I said. I hoped he wasn't going to drop his trousers and show me how big his willy was after getting. If he did, I was ready to pull on it with the hurl, and drive it up in the bushes for the magpies to collect. For feck's sake what's wrong with you? I says. Have you a fit of the shits or what?

Just come on till I show you something, says he.

Back up the road we went, in Mrs Rourke's gate and through the yard.

Ah, Mikey, not this caper again, says I. Go on in there yourself, if you want; I'm going up to the street. There were better things to be doing than gawping at Doran and the old Rourke one going hammer and tongs in the bed. Watching them was of no more interest; not since I'd found out what went on between men and women. Anyway, I was sick of all the spying carry-on for a pastime.

Any more of that and you'll be fit to be taken, I says to him.

Just one look inside, that's all. We won't be a minute, says he. I only want to show you this. It's different from the last time, and it won't take a second. I promise. He could be persuasive, Mikey, when he wanted his own way.

So, there we were back to the old tiptoe through the tulips caper. In the doorway we slipped, nobody

in the kitchen, and straight over to the door in the partition.

Yes, we're in business, says he, pointing. The voices were muffled inside. Mikey was in front of me at the door. He opened it gently and so slightly you'd hardly notice, even if your eyes were fixed on it. As he did, he stooped down, and I was able to look in over him.

She was underneath this time, her red hair splayed out. One of her hands rested on the pillow: fingers slightly bent like in a holy picture. If that was Patsy Doran under the blankets, on top of her, he sure as hell had grown into a mighty carcass since the last time. A big Blackstairs bolster of a man. I was getting worried: if he were to spot us and take off after us, we'd have no hope of getting away. The size of him! I couldn't see his head at all; only one big long hairy leg sticking out to the side, uncovered. A mountain of blankets heaved up and down in the bed, like an earthquake. Seeing the pink candlewick bedspread again gave me a weird feeling. For a moment I thought I was right back to the last time we'd been there. And there was that very same smell. I pitied poor old Rourkie: the size of him on top of her. But I don't think she minded somehow, the smile she was wearing.

Then it all went wrong. Mikey, the little gouger, took to the giggling, and couldn't be stopped. He had the hand over his mouth, holding in the sound. I gave him a clout on the head to stay quiet, but that didn't stop him. I tried to turn and take myself out of there, but I couldn't. He was in my way, crawling round under my feet like a baby. Mikey then crept back from the door, and stretched out behind me. This was turning into a right dog's bollocks. Might only make things worse, I'm thinking, if I try to get by him or hop over him. I had to stay put.

Peeping in again, I saw that Mrs Rourke had become alert. She'd heard something and started tapping your man on the shoulder – real urgently, like.

What did Mikey, the little worm, do then, only reach out his hand from where he'd got to – crouched over to one side – and give the door a hoosh in. Oh shit! Her big round eyes were staring up at me in shock, her mouth open and her chin hanging down. It struck me then that she was the nearest thing in looks to an old jinnet Vronnie Byrne had one time. Jinnet-face must've thought I was Jack the fecking Ripper standing there ready to do her in with a hatchet or something.

Then this great head emerged from under the blankets, like a sea monster rising from the deep. It turned to look. Oh fuck! The big, thick, round head of him, with the great bushy eyebrows – I knew them eyebrows and that look. The scowl and the mad-dog eyes were glaring straight at me. For a moment, I was stuck to the spot, as paralytic as the worst drunkard ever staggered out of Murphy's above – but only for a moment. Then I took off like sheet lightning. Out the door, out the yard, out the gate and up the road I ran as hard as ever I could, back up that road home, to the others, towards safety. I pushed it for all I was worth before them long naked legs could climb into their trousers and come galloping up behind me. I never once looked back. Any moment I'd hear him hot on my heels. But I made it home.

It didn't bother me one bit where Mikey, the treacherous little cunt, had taken himself to, or if he'd been caught. I hoped he was caught. But probably not, the minute the cute hoor had pushed the door wide, leaving me in the open, he was more than likely off tiptoeing into the back room. He'd have slipped in under the big table with the white tablecloth draped down over the sides, where no one would see him or think of looking. Mikey would've hidden there till it was safe to come out.

They were all out: Mam, Ciss, little Jimmy and Aidan. Mam was gone to my aunt's with Ciss and Jimmy. Heaven knows where Aidan was: off straying somewhere, like a buck-cat with the horn. No time to think where to hide till they'd get back, and no safe place where he wouldn't find me.

The top of my chest was thumping and tightening. I wanted to collapse on to the couch and do nothing till I'd get my breath back. Only then did the thought hit me: maybe I should've run in the other direction when I came out of Rourke's, and gone to the street. But he'd definitely catch up with me that way; it was such a long road. With all the panic I wasn't thinking straight. The best thing was to act normally, find something to do and get busy on it – right away – so all of that other matter might be brushed aside when he came in, like none of it ever happened. What if it hadn't happened, and was only a bad dream that I'd wake up from at any minute? I could still hear my chest pounding.

I grabbed the white enamel bucket – it was only half empty – and headed out to the draw-well for water. It was only within the last year that I'd started going for the water – to lend Mam a hand. Still not thinking straight, I fidgeted and foostered with the bucket, moving it about on the ground, steadying it. What was I doing? It was steady enough the way it was.

I had just about managed to get the well door open and turn the handle to unwind the iron bucket when he landed. I felt my shoulders shiver, and I sucked in air as if it was freezing. He was at the top of the yard, heading for the house. The moment he saw me, he stopped in his tracks and started coming over, real slow. I went on minding what I was doing, lowering the bucket, pretending nothing, but shaking. From the corner of my eye, I could see him watching me, as if I was some sort of vermin about to bolt, while he was ready to sprint across and cut me off, no matter what direction I might take.

The fear got worse. Each limb went zing quiver, like a frigging fiddle string. Every last blessed bone in my body shook. He stood over me like a towering great ogre. He'd never looked so tall and so menacing. I still went on pretending nothing, though the effort was nearly too great. I had this urge to look at him and catch his eye, as much as to say: move your carcass out of my way. But I wouldn't provoke him or rise his dirty temper.

I remembered what Father Breen had said, one time off the pulpit, about anger and turning the other cheek. Says he: Turning the other cheek means not antagonizing people who are in a state of crazy rage; taking care not to drive them berserk any more than they already are, and not to square up to them. The thing to do is turn away and allow them time to calm down. I never understood what the man used to go on about of a Sunday morning. The reason why that sermon had made any sense to me was because he was on about rage. I reckoned I knew all about tempers and cursed madness.

Right at that moment, more than ever, I needed to know what to do, and how not to drive the man psycho. I didn't want the going-over that I was sure lay ahead of me. I certainly didn't want his dirty shovel maulers near me that he'd been using to scrawb the tits off old jinnet-face half an hour before. Talk about rage! The man was seething. He was like the black kettle inside on the crane with far too much fire under it, boiling up, ready to burst out all over the place. I knew it the moment he opened his beak.

If you as much as hint to your mother, ever, what

you saw today, I'll kill you. If you as much as say anything, ever, to anyone about it, I'll kill you. He growled low, between his teeth, like a snarling dog before it attacks. He was holding back, ready to lunge. I kept tilting my head sideways, expecting the first thump to land.

By now I had got the galvanized bucket, full of water, wound up to the top. I was pulling it out from over the well, having let go of the winding handle, when I heard him growl again: Do you hear me? I heard him all right; I wasn't fucking deaf. Still I pretended nothing, kept on minding what I was doing, not once lifting my head. Do you hear me? he shrieked. This time it was that awful roar from the past: the time he'd chased Mam with the slop bucket, and I jumped in a start, spilling some of the water. I still didn't answer him. The heat under the kettle was getting turned up even higher.

I'd just about got a firm hold on the bottom of the bucket with the other hand, ready to pour the water into the white bucket for the house. That's when the buzzing in my ears started up, and my old friends, the grey dots, came floating before my eyes. A surge of rage went right through my body, this thing inside my head went click, and all that notion of patience and turning the other cheek flew out the window, quick as a dipping swallow on a rainy day. I simply wasn't able to keep it up any longer.

Every ounce of strength I had went into action. I let fly with the bucket, water and all, aimed high for the head – always the place to go to do the most damage. The bucket got him right in the face, and knocked him back on his arse on the ground. Water went splashing in all directions.

But there was no chance to savour my handiwork. The bucket bounced back towards the well because it was tied to the rope. I saw it coming but couldn't get out of the way in time, and it caught me on the forehead. The rim round the bottom, as it spun over, was what did the job. It knocked me off balance. I was half dazed but tried to grab the winding handle, the frame, the door . . . I missed all of them. There was nothing I could do. I fell in; went down.

Everything drifted past so slowly. The brown wet stones in the wall the colour of Mam's eyes, and the bits of sickly green fern that ought never to have been there in the first place: all went up by me. I could easily make out the marks in the stones the bucket had made, clattering down off them over the years. Below a certain point there were no more stones to be seen – solid cut rock the whole way down. The last person there was probably the first; the one who'd hammered and picked his way through – his scratches and scrawbs clear cut as if he'd been there only yesterday. How long did it take him? How much salty sweat and blood did he lose? He had to have been a small man to work with so little room. It was like I'd got to meet him, all of a sudden.

The light was disappearing back out through the hole where the door was, away at the top, like it was being sucked out by some great light pump. It got dark so quickly – black shagging dark. The falling, though, went on for ages: one, two, three . . . Like in a dream: the same queasy thing in the stomach – that never-ending, dropping-down feeling. Once again there was counting in my head: the sound of a father's voice, from long ago, counting between the flash and the clap: one, two, three . . . Next, the thump off the rock there jutting out, against my head.

And that was it. Lights out.

18

I WISH FATHER BREEN WOULD HURRY UP, SHIFT HIS backside off the seat there inside the vestry, and take himself out here quick. Everyone's sitting in their places, fretting, and waiting for him to make a start. No reason now for this delay. The usual stragglers have made it into the church, all here.

There goes that chorus again, clearing their throats, and old Vronnie is the ringleader. They're in full swing, boy: tut tut tut tutting away there in mad spates, getting ready to make speeches. Are they really coughing at all or is there more to it, like? Maybe it's a type of code they've worked out between them, to occupy the time and secretly chat to each other while sitting in the church.

Tut tut tut . . . oh hello, Vronnie, tut tut . . . how are you keeping? Tut tut . . . Tut tut tut . . . oh hello, Maggie, sure not too bad at all thanks, 'cept for the arthritis; it has my poor old body gone into a right cripple altogether, and my arse is sore sitting. Wouldn't you think his reverence would hurry up and not be keeping us locked up here all day. Oh! Maggie, have you any more, tut tut, strange for me? Have you nothing fresh on that Jane Rourke and Jimmy Cullen business? The old memory is gone to the dogs with me; can't remember a blessed thing nowadays. Wasn't it an awful thing to happen, though?

There's nothing at all, do you know, the matter with that one's memory. She just likes having the same old gossip told to her, over and over; she has to savour every last drop of it.

It's me, right now, has the trouble remembering things. I can remember nothing of hitting the water at the bottom of the well, or of ever waking up again before the end. Or much of the carry-on at the top: those last few minutes. It seems now the whole thing happened a hundred years ago, it's all so hazy. Snippets come flashing back all right but they're gone again in the blink of an eye, the way Long Johnny Codd has trouble sometimes keeping the reels running. All the stopping and starting, you'd end up seeing only scraps of a film, without any idea as to the hang of the story. That's what it's like with those last few minutes: they appear in bits and pieces. The whole picture never really comes together all at once to make sense. The only thing real about it now is the fear. I can still feel that; it's as powerful as ever.

The men must have spent hours there on their bellies, stretched in over the edge, while their hands shaded their eyes squinting down into the dark. The whole place was probably covered in ropes, grappling hooks and bits of tackle; the fishing and foostering going on endlessly. Raise, plunge and drag over, then back, trying for a grip. Not an easy job: handling those irons from such a height in so tight a space. They probably knocked off the John Players, flicked burnt matches at each other out of boredom, and sent empty gold-leaf-lined fag boxes spinning across the yard to hit against tall stalks of ragweed. Those cheeky nuisances of ragweed stick up all over the place: too brazen – like the ferns down the well – for their own good. Too fond of growing on stony ground.

I wonder how long it'll be before they get to reuse the well water for the house. I'd say weeks at least.

It'll mean all that traipsing across the fields again to the old spring well, and the long trudge back with two bucketfuls – only half full, though, on arrival. No doubt they'll keep on using the same white enamel bucket. Why not? That'll be Aidan's job. It'll drag the arms out of him, the fecker – and that it may. He'll more than likely bring Ciss with him to carry the gallon can for scooping up water. She'd better be careful, though, to skim the flies and scum off the top first, and not stir up mud from the bottom. There's a knack in that.

Aidan was right. He always said we should've sunk a well for an electric pump ages ago and got the running water in, same as in most other places nowadays. But would Old Shagsticks hear of it? That might only make life too easy. Maybe he'll think about it now, and get in the Aga as well. He might bargain that cooker off your one below on the hill. If he has time, like, and he's not too busy bargaining other things off her. Just imagine, hot running water inside the house. Well, feck me! They might get in a bath and maybe even a television.

He was always dead nuts against television. He says it only corrupts people – whatever that means. I suppose he thinks no work would get done round the place: too much time would get spent sitting inside. But then again, who's to say?

Come on now, Father, let's get this show on the road here, and we'll have everything over and done with in no time. People have homes to go to, you know; can't expect them to spend all day sitting in the church, gawking. And all the prayers that have to be got through! So let's get a move on. I swear, the man would keep you locked up all day if he could get away with it: he's nothing short of a bloody sadist. Oh, right so, here he is now; let's give him a round of applause.

Out he marches through the vestry door, the servers ahead of him, over to the first step of the altar. Straight away he launches into the prayers. That's it, Father, that's the job, keep her stirring, Patsy boy. You were always a right one, weren't you, when you got going? I used to love the sound of that old Latin: *Introibo ad altare Dei* . . . But they've gone and changed it. Why don't they leave things alone, especially the good bits?

Hey, Father, did you see that? Someone's left a flower on the coffin lid. That's queer odd, though, ain't it? Well, they bloody well broke themselves: one mangy flower. Excuse me now, Father, for interrupting, but I can't let that go. I'll be only a second.

Mogue Doyle

Hey there, my dear brethren – did I say that right now, Father, did I? Listen up now, I'm giving the sermon here today. Who's the hoor with the flower famine in his garden this year, well? One single miserable blasted flower. What's the name of this most generous individual?

But wait now . . . Isn't it very like the scrawny roses that grow out over the wall on the hill below? Same as the one I stuck in the keyhole, of a Sunday afternoon, not a million years ago. Where's Mrs Paleface sitting, till I have a chat with her: there's things I want to ask that woman. Now, Father, on second thoughts, maybe I'll leave this business of the sermon to you.

The Mass doesn't take that long now after all. It's the waiting at the start that's the killer; sitting and expecting something new and strange, while knowing full well that nothing's going to happen. Nothing that hasn't happened before. No new excitement to keep you on the edge of your seat. Yet everybody, mouths open, always sits gawping, like the pictures were going to start up.

Well, is this it then, over and done with? Hey, Vronnie, how is your old arse now? Is it still sore?

Come on there, lads, get that coffin on its way; let's start moving it down the aisle. We haven't all frigging day; no time now for a tea break. You're not working for the council, you know. There's a burial to be got through. Let's get on with it then and not stand around moping like zombies. Has the smell of incense gone to your heads or what?

Well, seeing as yous are like that about it, I'm not going to hang around here any longer. Yous can have it all to yourselves now, lads. I'm on my way. The show's over. Got other things on my plate. That's it, Father, give that thurible a right good rattle there; fumigate the place and kill the smell of farts. I always love to soak up that spicy incense when it comes wafting through the air. Look at the way it spumes out when he jingle-jangles the chain, soft puffs of smoke drifting in waves over the coffin, like it was going to soak up the wood into its whiteness.

Mrs Brennan is outside tearing like a sputnik along the pebblestone path from the priest's house, to get to the bell. Thar she blows now, with her arse cocked out, ready to start pulling like a Trojan. A right one for the job, ain't she?

I don't suppose there's any use having a quick word with Minnie before I go. I only want to whisper a word in her ear: a few tips, like, on how to handle Mr Rocket-man himself, Aidan; and how to avoid him jumping on her every time he sees her, like the red rooster at home that thinks he's got a whole flock of Rhode Island Reds to get through treading before nightfall.

Hey, Minnie, how's about a bit of an old-time waltz there? Just you and me; one last dance – one for the road – what? It's my turn to curtsey and bow, you know, this time. Let that bendy-river music flow. Ah! This is the job, away we go: WAN two three, WAN two three, WAN two three . . .

Da da daa daa daa daa,

Da daa, da daa . . .

Da da daa daa daa daa, da da deeee . . .

Ah Mam! Must say goodbye to Mam before I go. Can't though; I just can't. I can't stand seeing her face: that look on it again. How old she's got all of a sudden – that's the worst of all. She's a different person; not like the woman I know. Those awful false teeth do nothing for her; only make her look like death warmed up: a full set of gleaming crockery in a shrunken face. I don't want to see that. I wish I could put everything back right, just for her sake. To see her sparkle into life, the old life of long ago. The way she was then is how I want to remember her; the only way to remember her. But there's no going back on things. It's too late for all that. Too fucking late.

The clapper falls. Clang . . . I feel the pull. Hey, Brudgie, I don't suppose you want to come on a little trip with me? We'd make good music together, me and you. I'll show you how to dance. What do you think? Well, all right then – deaf as a doornail, that one, when she wants to be.

Another clang: that bell again. Pulling me with it . . . Away. Out over Murphy's and the village, down along the valley, across the river and up the other side to the flat townlands beyond; where the big farmers keep their pot-bellied cattle lounging in the long grass, luscious long grass. I'd love to lie down and rest a while here, and listen to those cattle chomping on the green stalks and chewing the cud at their ease. Like listening to the sheep grazing, the night of the row with Patsy Doran.

Is there another mountain beyond this? Well now, that's the way it goes. Up she flew and . . . See you later, alligator; in a while, crocodile. See you later, alligator . . .

Acknowledgements

The author and publishers are grateful for permission to reproduce the following lyrics:

On page 37, words by Lennon & McCartney taken from the song 'From Me To You'. By kind permission of Northern Songs/Sony ATV Music Publishing.

On page 143, 'Do Wah Diddy Diddy' by Jeff Barry and Ellie Greenwich – © 1963 by Trio Music Co. Inc. – All Rights Reserved – Lyric reproduced by kind permission of Carlin Music Corp., London NW1 8BD.

On page 149, 'Alexander's Ragtime Band', Words and Music by Irving Berlin © 1911 Irving Berlin Inc., USA, B. Feldman & Co. Ltd, London WC2H 0QY. Reproduced by permission of International Music Publications Ltd. All Rights Reserved.